Warriors
of the Ancient World

Warriors
of the Ancient World

MARTIN J. DOUGHERTY

amber
BOOKS

Published by
Amber Books Ltd
74–77 White Lion Street
London
N1 9PF
United Kingdom
www.amberbooks.co.uk
Appstore: itunes.com/apps/amberbooksltd
Facebook: www.facebook.com/amberbooks
Twitter: @amberbooks

ISBN: 978-1-78274-446-7

Project Editor: Michael Spilling
Designer: Zoe Mellors
Picture Research: Terry Forshaw

Printed in China

Picture Credits
AKG: 12tl (JH-Lightbox/John Hies), 53r (Erich Lessing), 98/99, 106/107
AKG/Peter Connolly: 24/25, 28/29, 32b, 34/35, 38l, 44b, 56, 78/79, 82, 84/85, 85, 89, 96/97, 104, 107, 113l, 122b
AKG/Giuseppe Rava: 7, 60, 68/69, 86, 114/115
Alamy: 1 (Stephen Mulcahey), 9r (Interfoto), 10t (Biblelandpictures), 11 (HIP), 12tr (Imagestate), 12b (Art Archive), 13 (Lebrecht), 15 (Andrew Warburton), 16r (Art Archive), 17r (Dorling Kindersley), 22 (VPC Travel Photo), 26/27 (Peter Horree), 30/31 (Nikolay Vinokurov), 32t (Interfoto), 38/39 (Wyrdlight), 44t (Image Broker), 45 (Jochen Tack), 46b (Ancient Art & Architecture), 48 (Atlaspix), 65 (Biblelandpictures), 66/67 (Robert Harding), 72/73 (Harris Vithoulkas), 76 (Art Archive), 76/77 (National Geographic), 79 (Interfoto), 82/83 (Stephen Mulcahey), 105 (Art Archive), 110/111 (National Geographic), 112 (Nick Turner), 118/119 (Atlaspix), 120 (Cultura RM), 121 (HIP)
Alamy/A. F. Archive: 8, 14/15, 18/19, 40/41, 49, 70/71, 88, 90/91, 102/103, 122t, 123
Amber Books: 6/7, 36/37, 62/63, 80/81, 94/95, 116/117, 125
Bridgeman/Look & Learn: 61, 92/93, 100/101, 108/109
Corbis: 52 & 53r (Thorne Anderson), 74/75 (Outline/Steve Schapiro), 124/125 (Nathan Benn)
Depositphotos: 16l (Anatoly Vartanov), 21 (Anastasios71), 43 (Paul Fleet), 47 (Luis Louro), 101 (Ileana_bt), 113r both (3d Renders)
Dorling Kindersley: 66t
Dreamstime: 10 (Windowseat), 42/43 (Dzain), 50 (Swisshippo), 57 (Maisna), 66b (Jose I. Soto)
Fotolia: 33 (Cyril Comtat)
Getty Images: 46t (UIG), 51 (AFP/Oli Scarff), 54 (Gianni Dagli Orti), 55 (Hulton), 58 (Jeremy Sutton-Hibbert), 58/59 (AFP/Oli Scarff), 64 (Hulton)
Getty Images/De Agostini: 9l, 10b, 17l, 23, 25, 87

CONTENTS

THE ANCIENT WORLD

Ancient history began with the Ancient Egyptians in around 3,500 BCE. It lasted until the end of the Roman Empire in the fifth century CE. Many great civilizations rose and fell in this period, including the Assyrians, Greeks and Persians.

The Roman Empire lasted from 509 BCE until 476 CE. At its height, it stretched from Britain in the northwest to Parthia in modern-day Iran.

Above: Barbarians from central Asia swept across Europe and eventually helped destroy the Roman Empire.

Left: The battles mentioned in the book are marked on the map.

CHAPTER 1

WARRIORS

In the ancient world, the leaders of each land fought beside their warriors. Kings solved their problems by defeating their enemies in battle.

Left: Simple hand weapons like these were deadly in a hand-to-hand battle.

Below: Helmets like this one, from Greece, protected against a blow to the head.

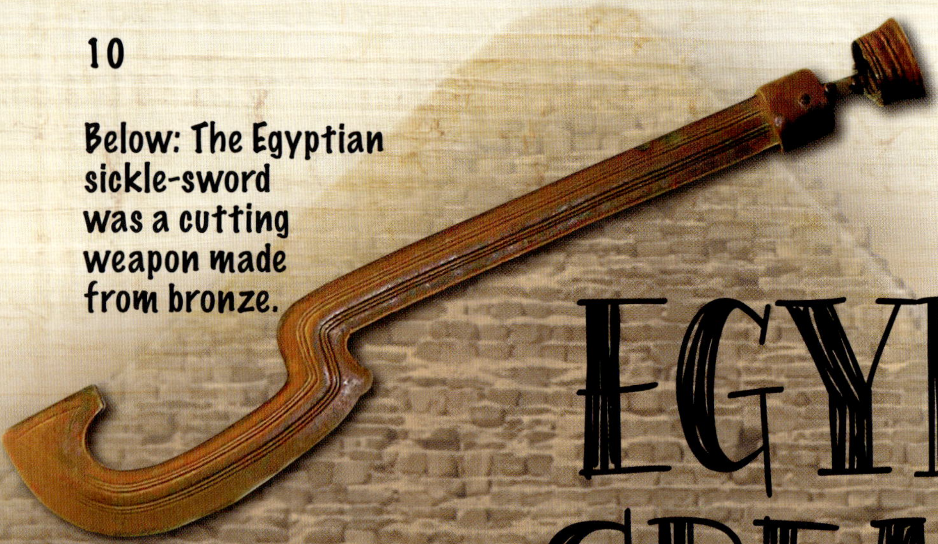

Below: The Egyptian sickle-sword was a cutting weapon made from bronze.

EGYPTIAN SPEARMEN

ANCIENT EGYPT

Ancient Egypt was one of the first civilizations, dating from 3000 BCE. It had to fight for survival against enemies who came from all directions.

- Egyptian kings were called pharaohs and were skilled war leaders.
- Egypt defeated many enemies before being conquered by the Romans.

Right: Daggers in Egypt were made of bronze and often had ivory handles.

The Ancient Egyptians beat their enemies by being well organised. Their commanders could move around blocks of soldiers to outwit their enemies.

2000 – 1000 BCE

Skilled Spearmen

Most Egyptian soldiers were armed with a spear and a shield, and they had daggers for up-close fighting. Soldiers stood closely together so they could fight as a unit and help each other.

Below: Egyptian spearmen fought in blocks, as this model shows.

PERSIAN IMMORTALS

The Persian Empire relied on its elite force, called the Immortals, to defeat all enemies.

Best Job in the Empire

The Immortals got the best food and were looked after by servants. Their job was dangerous but well rewarded. Many people wanted to be one of the Immortals.

Top: The people of the Persian Empire showed how important the Immortals were by carving images of them in stone.

Right: The Immortals were also honoured by paintings that showed their spears, bows and clothing.

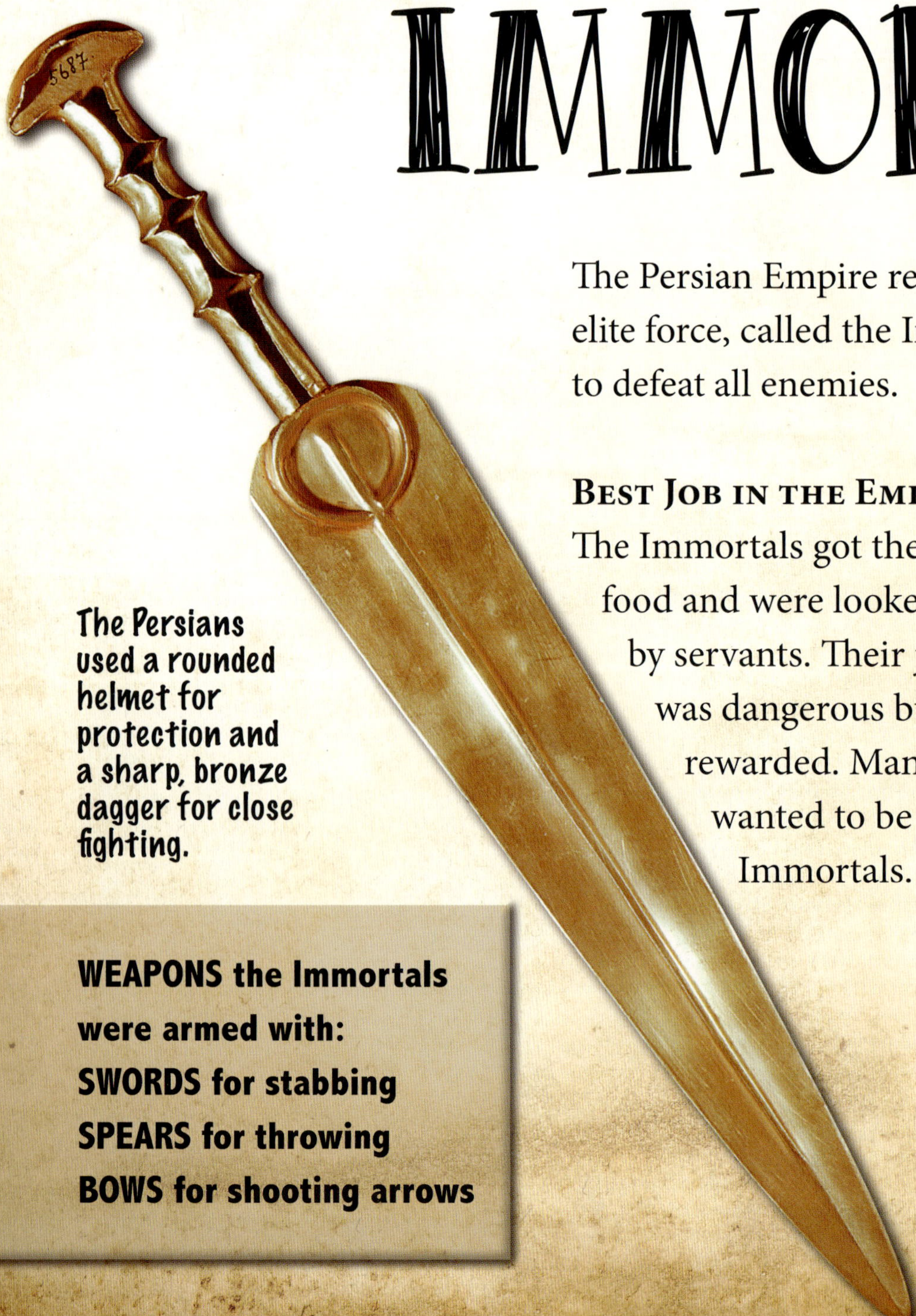

The Persians used a rounded helmet for protection and a sharp, bronze dagger for close fighting.

WEAPONS the Immortals were armed with:
SWORDS for stabbing
SPEARS for throwing
BOWS for shooting arrows

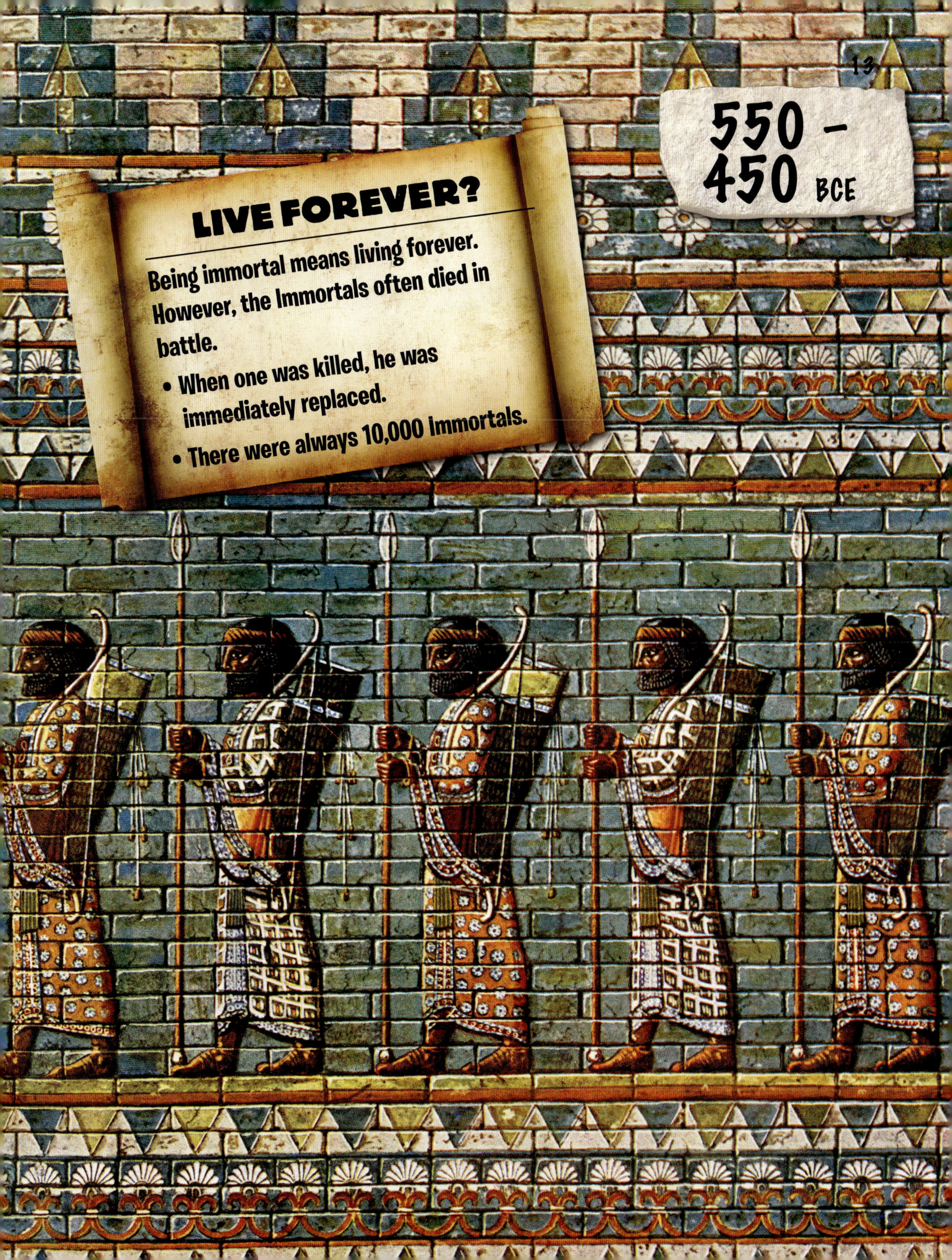

550 – 450 BCE

LIVE FOREVER?

Being immortal means living forever. However, the Immortals often died in battle.

- When one was killed, he was immediately replaced.
- There were always 10,000 Immortals.

700 - 200 BCE

GREEK HOPLITES

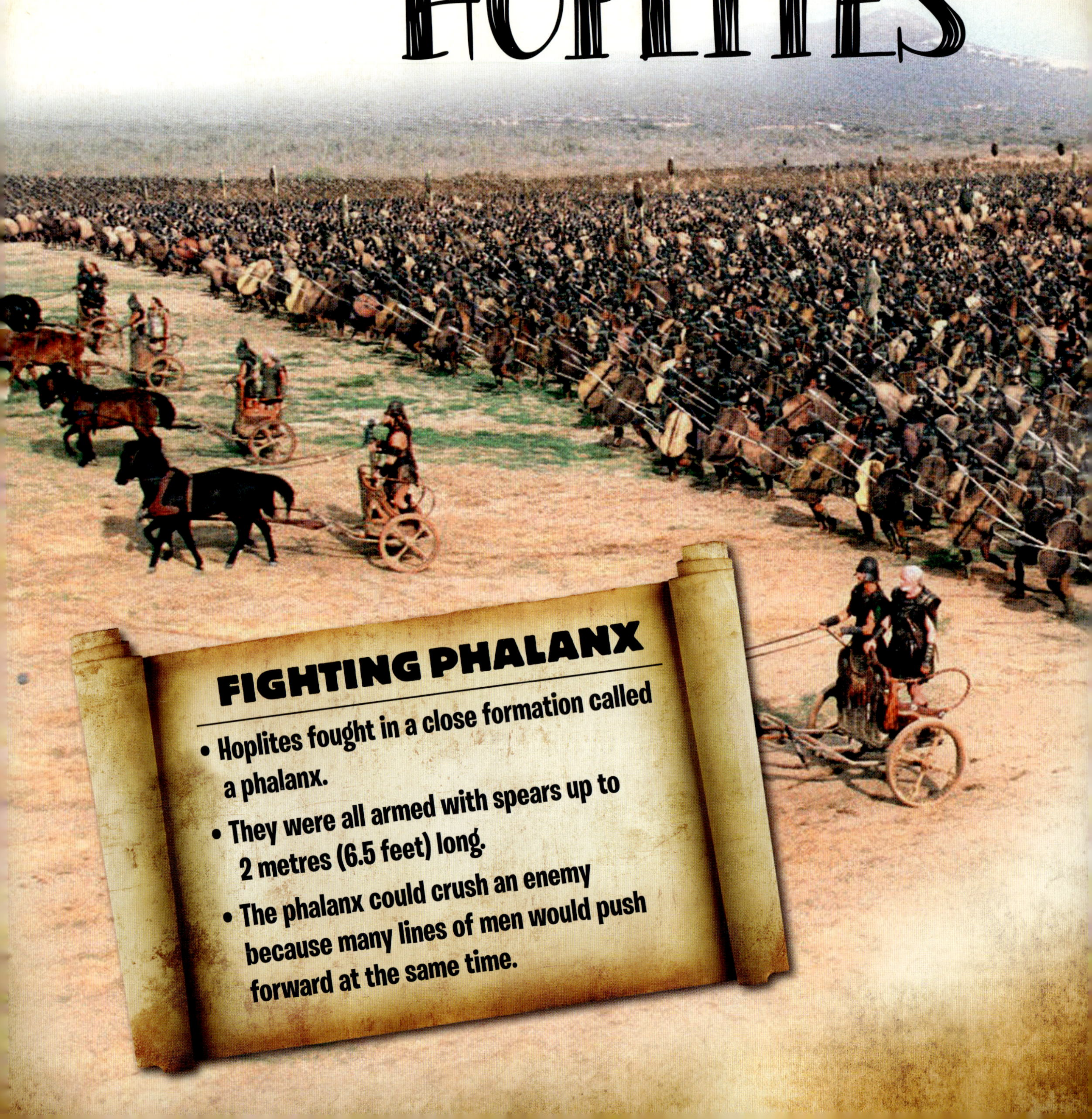

FIGHTING PHALANX

- Hoplites fought in a close formation called a phalanx.
- They were all armed with spears up to 2 metres (6.5 feet) long.
- The phalanx could crush an enemy because many lines of men would push forward at the same time.

Below: With their leaders at the front sitting in chariots, an army of hoplites enter battle.

Ancient Greek armies were mostly made up of hoplites. These were spearmen who carried large shields for protection. Some also wore armour and helmets.

DID YOU KNOW?

The word 'hoplite' comes from *hoplon*, which is the name of the round shield they used.

ARMOUR AND WEAPONS

HELMET

Bronze was used for headgear.

BREASTPLATE

Bronze armour protected the chest.

HELMET

Greek helmets protected the head and face well but still let the warrior see and breathe.

SWORD
Greek swords were usually 50 centimetres (20 inches) long and made of iron.

The Ancient Greeks used armour and weapons made of bronze. This was a common metal which could be shaped with heat and hammers. Their armour and large shields were heavy but gave the Greeks protection from the arrows, swords and spears of their enemies.

SHIELD
A Greek warrior's shield was highly decorated. Losing it was a great shame, even if he survived the battle.

480 BCE

SPARTAN PHALANX

DID YOU KNOW?

The film *300* tells how the Spartans led other Greeks to defeat a powerful Persian army.

PHALANX IN ACTION

- The first three ranks would point their spears at the enemy.
- They would overlap their shields to protect the group.

Sparta was one of the most important cities in Ancient Greece, and was known for its warlike ways.

Skilled Spartans

Spartan warriors were very tough and skilled. They fought in a traditional Greek phalanx formation and could defeat almost any enemy they came up against.

540 - 480 BCE

LEONIDAS WARRIOR KING

Leonidas was the king of the Spartans. He led the fight against invading Persians at the Battle of Thermopylae in 480 BCE. Leonidas led a force of a few hundred Greeks to hold back a massive Persian army for three days. This allowed the main Greek army to escape.

WINNING TACTICS

Leonidas was able to hold off a much larger Persian army by:

- defending a narrow path between a mountain and the sea
- packing his men tightly in the narrow space
- using his best fighters in the front rank

Right: Leonidas and almost all his men were killed, but they won the battle and stopped the invasion.

DID YOU KNOW?

Many Greek cities had their own kings. Wars between the cities were common.

1000 BCE

AMAZONS

In Greek legends, the Amazons were a tribe of women warriors who were extremely fierce in battle. Their favourite weapon was the battle-axe.

The Ancient Greeks believed that the Amazons were as skilled as male warriors. Some legends said that an Amazon could not get married until she had killed a man.

DID YOU KNOW?

The Amazons were so famous that their name is now used to describe any fierce female warrior or fighter.

WHERE DID THEY LIVE?

The Ancient Greeks told a lot of stories about the Amazons, but no one seemed to know where the Amazons lived.

- Some said the Amazons were from what is now northern Turkey.
- Others claimed they lived in northern Africa.

Left: The Greeks made many stone carvings that show Amazons defeating male Greek warriors in battle.

Below: The ancient artists often showed Amazons fighting on horseback.

MACEDONIAN PHALANX

Alexander's spearmen fought in a phalanx but used a spear called a *sarissa*, which was much longer than the earlier Greek spears.

Prickly Porcupine

A Macedonian phalanx was a wall of spear points marching forward – almost like a porcupine. This took a lot of practice and training to get right, but it made the Macedonians very dangerous on the battlefield.

ALEXANDER THE GREAT (356–323 BCE)

Alexander the Great was a king of Macedonia who defeated all other Greek kings. He then led the Greeks to conquer the vast Persian empire.

331 BCE

Right: Each Macedonian carried a *sarissa* that was about 5.5 m (18 feet) in length. This weapon was a kind of pike, or a pole with a sharp end.

331 BCE

BATTLE OF GAUGAMELA

DID YOU KNOW?

The Battle of Gaugamela took place in what is now modern-day Iraq.

At the battle of Gaugamela, Alexander the Great smashed a Persian army and defeated the Persian emperor Darius. Alexander went on to conquer Egypt, Persia, and even parts of India.

Short-lived Empire

Alexander was a brave leader who fought with his army, but his empire quickly broke up after he died.

SPEARS VERSUS ELEPHANTS

AT SPEAR'S LENGTH

- The long spears of the Macedonian phalanx allowed them to stab the attacking elephants while not getting too close.
- This tactic worked because the fighters stayed in a phalanx, and the elephants had a hard time harming individual soldiers.

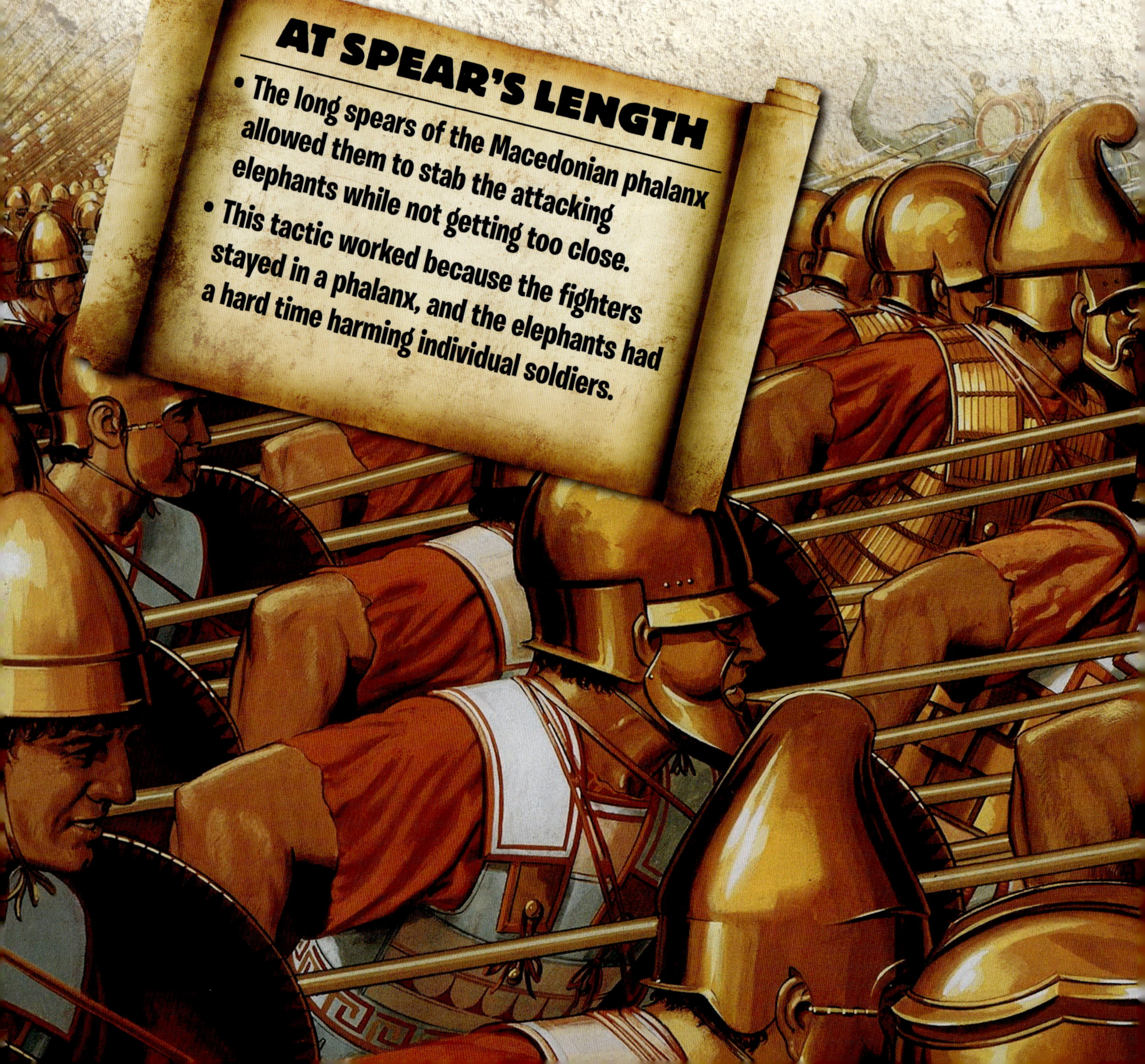

326 BCE

Alexander the Great's army reached India, where it came up against Indian armies that used war elephants. This was a new challenge for the Macedonian spearmen.

Brave Enemy

At the battle of Hydaspes in 326 BCE, Alexander's men took heavy casualties but won the battle. Alexander was so impressed with the bravery of his enemy, King Porus, that he let Porus keep his kingdom.

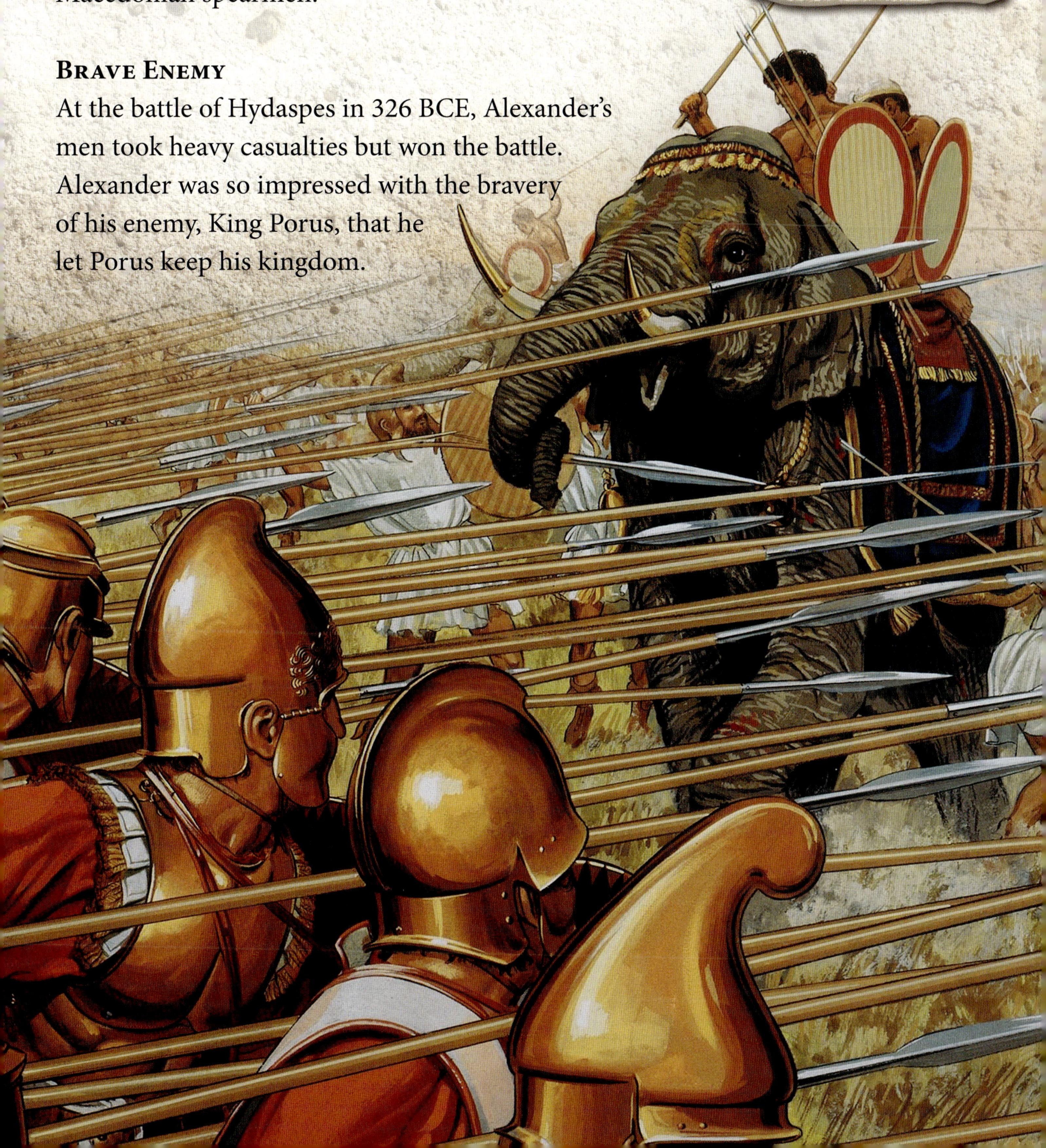

509 BCE – 200 CE

ROMAN LEGIONARIES

The Roman army was the best organised and trained in the ancient world. The Romans wore armour made of either chainmail or bands of metal called *lorica segmentata*, plus a helmet.

DID YOU KNOW?

A Roman legion normally had between 4,000 and 6,000 soldiers.

Legions

The Roman army was organised into legions, so Roman soldiers were called legionaries.

TOUGH FIGHTERS

Roman legionaries were tough fighters who worked closely together.

- They threw a javelin called a *pilum* and then closed in to fight with a short sword called a *gladius*.
- Romans were trained to help one another out and to gang up on their enemies.

DAGGER
Made of iron for stabbing.

ROMAN ARMOUR

Below: A Roman legionary had to clean and fix his armour. He had to sharpen his short sword (*gladius*) and spear (*pilum*).

The Roman army's equipment changed over time. If an enemy had a useful weapon, the Romans copied it or made their own version.

Chainmail and Armour

The Roman army used breastplates and armour of chainmail, which they copied from barbarians living in Gaul. However, the Romans were known for their *lorica segmentata*.

LORICA SEGMENTATA

- The *lorica segmentata*, or banded armour, was cleverly made from overlapping bands of metal.
- It took a long time to put on, but it let the soldier move freely.

LORICA SEGMENTATA

DID YOU KNOW?

Lorica segmentata **weighed roughly 9 kilograms (20 pounds).**

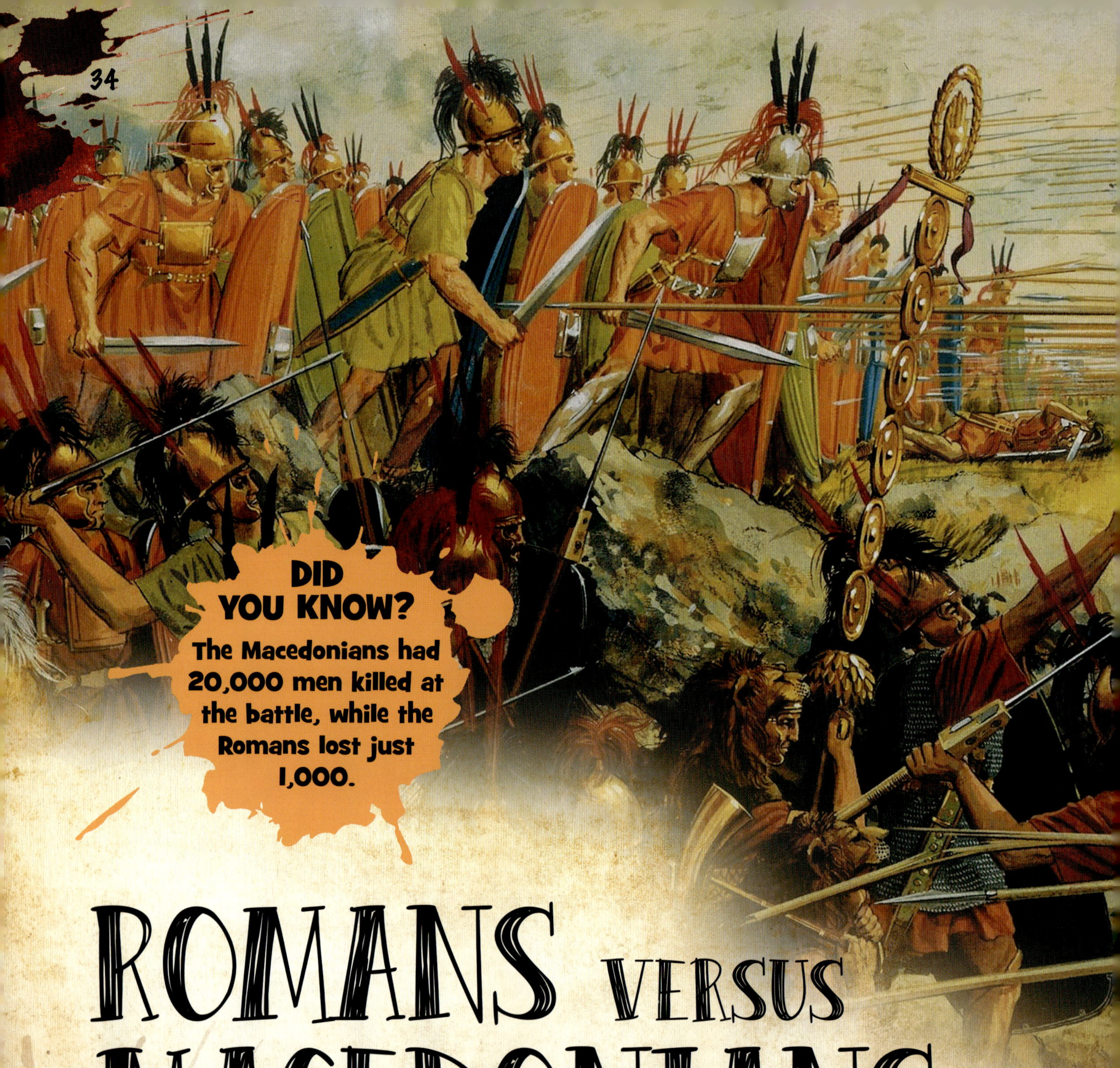

DID YOU KNOW?
The Macedonians had 20,000 men killed at the battle, while the Romans lost just 1,000.

ROMANS VERSUS MACEDONIANS AT PYDNA

At the battle of Pydna in 168 BCE, Roman legions met the phalanxes of Macedonia. Two of the best fighting forces in the world battled it out – and the Romans won.

168 BCE

Getting Close

The Romans found it hard to get past the spear points of the Macedonians, but once they got in close they could kill them with their short swords.

BROKEN PHALANX

When the Macedonians tried to move across rough ground, gaps opened in their phalanx, letting the Romans charge in.

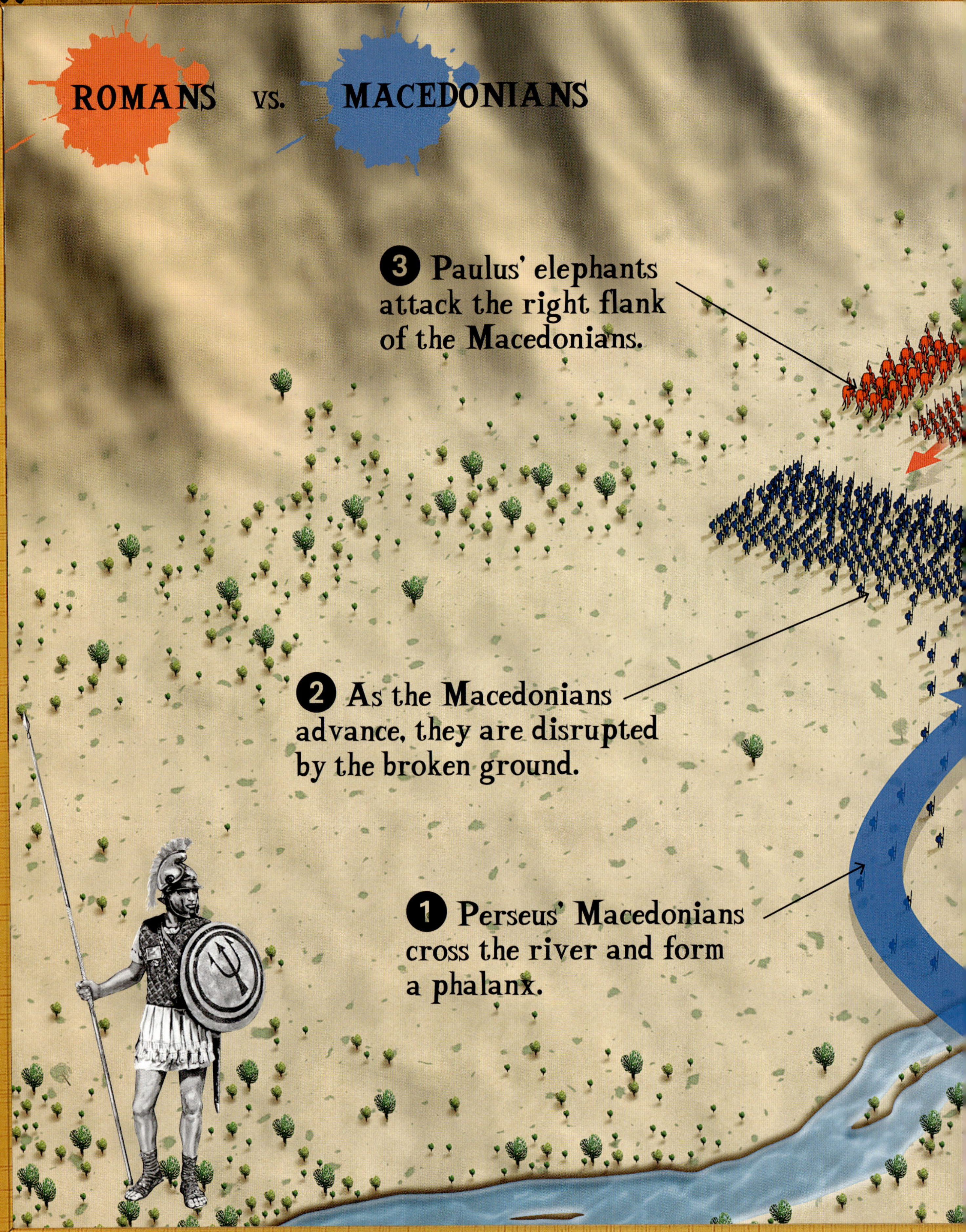
ROMANS vs. MACEDONIANS
3 Paulus' elephants attack the right flank of the Macedonians.
2 As the Macedonians advance, they are disrupted by the broken ground.
1 Perseus' Macedonians cross the river and form a phalanx.

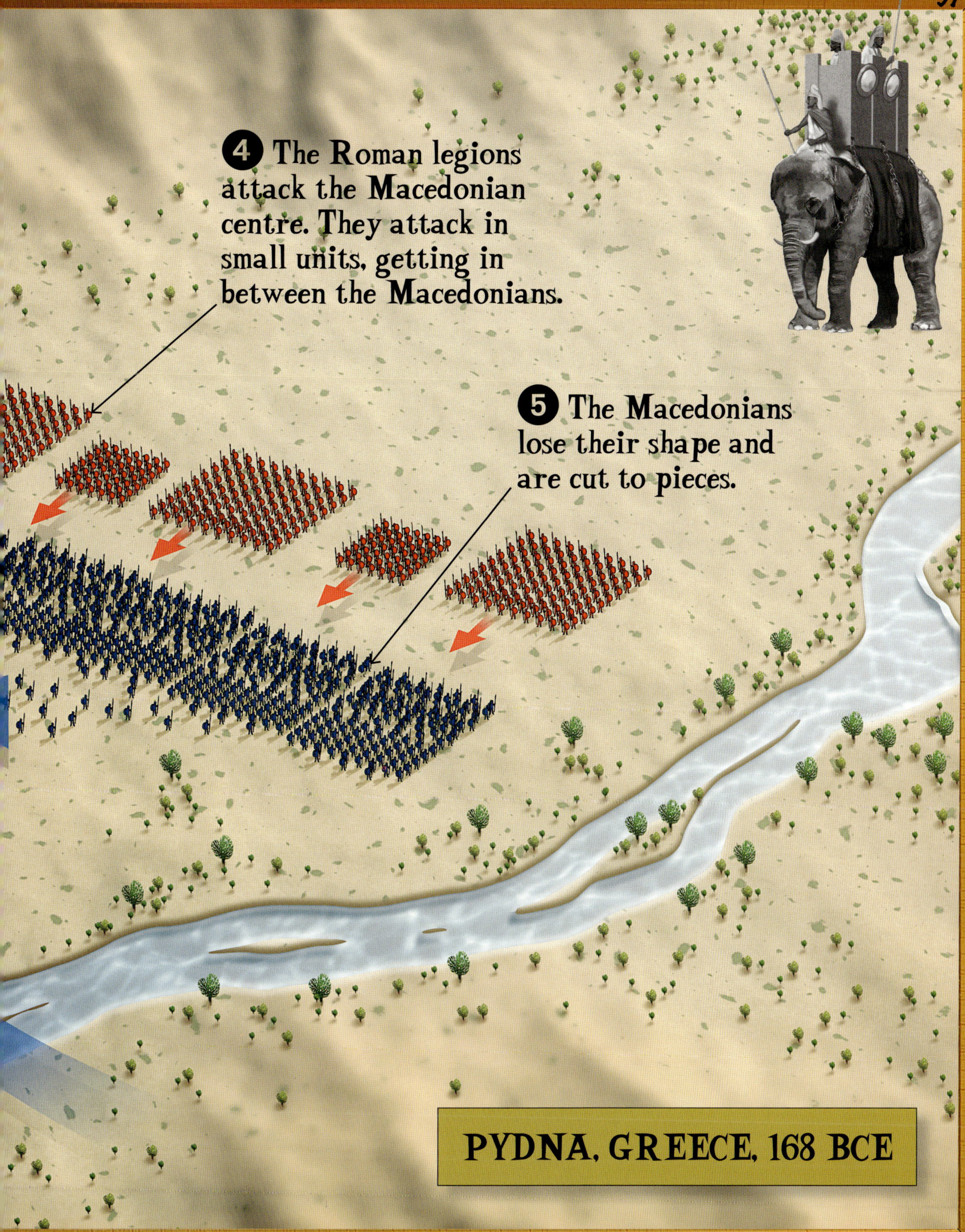
4 The Roman legions attack the Macedonian centre. They attack in small units, getting in between the Macedonians.
5 The Macedonians lose their shape and are cut to pieces.
PYDNA, GREECE, 168 BCE

ROMAN BATTLE STANDARDS

DID YOU KNOW?
It was a great honour to carry a standard – but also dangerous, since enemies would try to capture it.

TYPES OF STANDARD

Roman legions had several standards, each with different meanings.

- The *vexillum* was a small square flag that showed the name of the legion.
- The *imago* was an image of the emperor, which supposedly watched over the legion.

Roman Eagle

Roman soldiers were very proud of their standards. The most important was the Eagle, usually made from bronze or silver.

ROMAN FIGHTING SKILLS

When they needed to, Roman soldiers could close ranks and overlap their shields, making it very difficult for an enemy to hit them. The Romans could drive back their foes by bashing them with shields or by stabbing them with short swords. When the enemy started to fall back, the legion could open up its ranks to give each man more room to fight.

GLADIUS: short sword for stabbing
PILUM: long spear for stabbing and throwing
SCUTUM: large shield for defence and bashing

DID YOU KNOW?

A legionary did not need much room to use a *gladius* – so it worked well in close combat.

TESTUDO

The *testudo* or 'tortoise' was a clever way of using shields to create a moving fortress. Roman soldiers using this formation were protected against arrows and sling stones as they advanced toward the enemy.

Once they got close, the commander gave the order to open their ranks and attack, and the legion charged into action.

DID YOU KNOW?

Most arrows would just bounce off the shields with nothing more than a scary noise.

SCUTUM

- A scutum was 102 cm (40 inches) high and 41 cm (16 inches) wide.
- It would stand up on its own if placed on the ground.
- It was curved to cover the body.

A *scutum* was made of three sheets of wood glued together and covered with canvas and leather.

SHIELD

GLADIATORS

Above: A Roman stone carving, showing different types of gladiators fighting each other.

Gladiators were men who fought each other for sport and entertainment. They were watched by crowds of Romans in special arenas, who would cheer on their favourite gladiators. They would often fight to the death.

Warrior Style

Their costumes were based on weapons and armour used by Roman soldiers and their enemies.

GLADIATOR HELMETS

Gladiators wore many different types of helmet, including headgear that also protected the neck and chin.

Below: The weapons of the gladiators were dangerous, so re-enactors use safer versions to show how gladiators fought.

DID YOU KNOW?

Gladiators were usually slaves. If they fought well, they could gain their freedom.

BARBARIAN WARRIORS

Romans called many of their enemies 'barbarians'. The word comes from the Ancient Greeks, who thought that foreigners sounded as if they were talking nonsense, much like 'bar-bar-bar', when they spoke.

What most barbarian tribes had in common was that they were brave but not very well organised.

BARBARIAN WEAPONS

Barbarians would carry whatever kinds of weapons they could afford.

- Richer nobles would be armed with swords and wear armour.
- Poorer fighters would have clubs and use farming tools as weapons.

Above: This decorated shield was made by the Celts, who were great warriors.

Right: The swords of barbarian nobles were often simple in design.

400 BCE – 400 CE

DID YOU KNOW?

Barbarians were lone fighters who were very skilled in one-to-one combat.

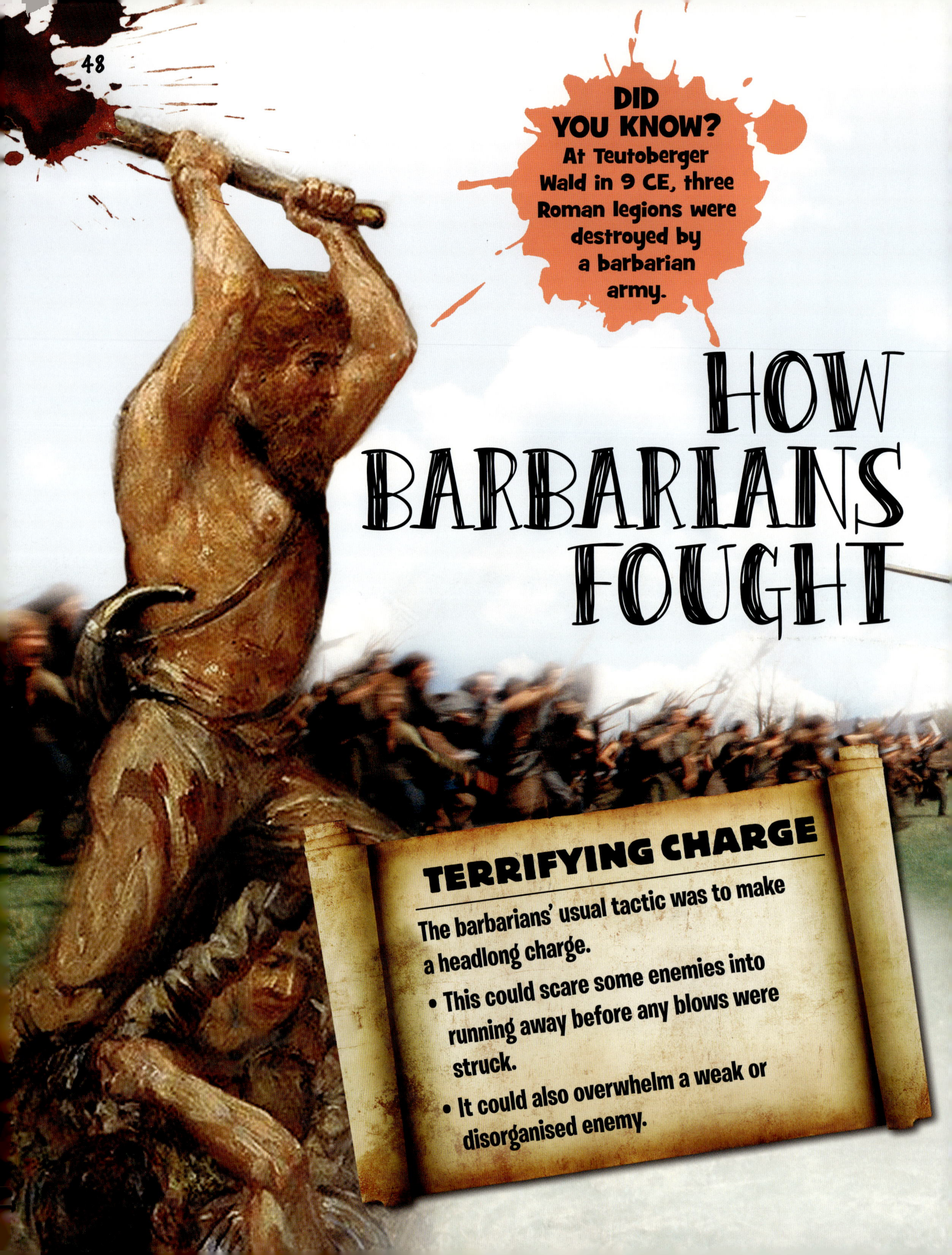

DID YOU KNOW?
At Teutoberger Wald in 9 CE, three Roman legions were destroyed by a barbarian army.

HOW BARBARIANS FOUGHT

TERRIFYING CHARGE

The barbarians' usual tactic was to make a headlong charge.

- This could scare some enemies into running away before any blows were struck.
- It could also overwhelm a weak or disorganised enemy.

Although they were fearsome warriors, the barbarians did not fight like an organised army. This allowed the Romans and others to beat the barbarian forces.

- Barbarians usually fought like heroes rather than soldiers, rushing to be the first to strike the enemy.
- The barbarians were not able to quickly recover from setbacks on the battlefield.

CHAPTER 2

MISSILE TROOPS

Striking the enemy from a distance was an important part of ancient warfare. Warriors used bows and slings, or threw spears at their enemies.

Left: These stone carvings show Assyrian archers shooting at the defenders of a city. Bowmen could attack enemies even if they hid behind strong walls.

Right: The Roman army used archers called *sagitarii* to support their legionaries with a hail of arrows.

1400 - 600 BCE

ASSYRIAN ARCHERS

SIEGE EXPERTS
Some enemies would not come out of their fortresses to fight, so the Assyrians had to become experts at siege warfare.

The Assyrian army was very well trained and organised. It rarely lost a battle even if the enemy outnumbered the Assyrian soldiers.

Curved Bows

The Assyrians used a recurve bow. This meant that the bow curved away from the archer. So when the bow was pulled against the curve, the archer had extra power for firing arrows.

ASSYRIAN EMPIRE

The Assyrian Empire conquered most of the Middle East. It almost collapsed but recovered many times over hundreds of years.

- The capital was at Assur (in modern-day Iraq).
- The most famous Assyrian king was Sargon of Akkad.

DID YOU KNOW?
The Assyrian Empire was spread across today's Iraq, Syria, Turkey, and Iran.

Below: Assyrian helmets were tall and cone-shaped to deflect blows. They were made of bronze.

DID YOU KNOW?

Homemade slings were used for hunting or to protect farms against wild animals.

Left: The Assyrian army used slings as well as bows. Assyrian slingers also carried swords.

SLINGERS

The sling was a cheap and simple weapon that was used to fling a small stone with incredible speed and power.

Lots of Practice!

Hitting a moving target with a sling was difficult and needed constant practice.

USING A SLING

Slings were hard to use but had some big advantages.

- A sling was easy to carry.
- Ammunition for firing could be found lying on the ground!

Right: In the Bible, the shepherd David killed the mighty warrior Goliath with a sling.

FIGHTING WITH A PILUM

PILUM FACTS

- Thrown by a strong arm, a *pilum* had a range of 33 metres (100 feet).
- It was about 2 m (6 feet 5 inches) long.
- It weighed 3 kilograms (7 pounds).

DID YOU KNOW?

A *pilum* that hit an enemy's shield would weigh it down and make it difficult to use.

Roman soldiers were trained to throw their *pila* (javelins) just before making contact with the enemy. This could break up an enemy charge if the Romans were defending, or make holes in the enemy line for the Romans to charge into with their swords.

ROMAN ARCHERS

The Roman army was famous for its legionaries, who were swordsmen. But they also used other types of troops, such as archers, to help them in battle.

The Roman army was highly organised. Its *sagitarii*, or archers, could shoot many arrows into an enemy force, weakening its ability to fight when the legionaries charged into action.

Left: Some Roman archers were heavily armoured to protect them against the swords and arrows of the enemy.

400 BCE – 400 CE

DID YOU KNOW?

Roman archers could hit targets at a maximum range of about 230 m (250 yards).

ARCHER POWER

At first the Romans paid foreign archers to serve in their armies, but soon they began to train their own.

- About one in every three Roman archers was mounted on a horse.
- Roman archers would often shoot fire arrows at their enemies, especially if they were in a wooded area.

250 BCE – 200 CE

PARTHIAN HORSE ARCHERS

The Parthians were fierce warriors from the Middle East. They were among the toughest enemies the Romans ever faced.

Defeat at Carrhae

At the Battle of Carrhae in 53 BCE, a Roman army was defeated by Parthians who shot thousands of arrows at the Romans from horseback.

Below: The Romans' shields gave them some protection. At Carrhae, however, they had few archers with them, so they could not strike back at the Parthians.

DID YOU KNOW?
The Parthians could turn round in the saddle and shoot back at someone behind them.

MENACING MISSILES

Horse archers were very dangerous, even though they wore little or no armour to protect themselves.

- They could get into range to shoot their bows very quickly.
- If they got tired or were in danger they could ride away.

Above: The fast-moving Parthian horse archers could shoot at the Romans from a distance of about 65 m (70 yards). They would not come within reach of the Romans' swords and spears.

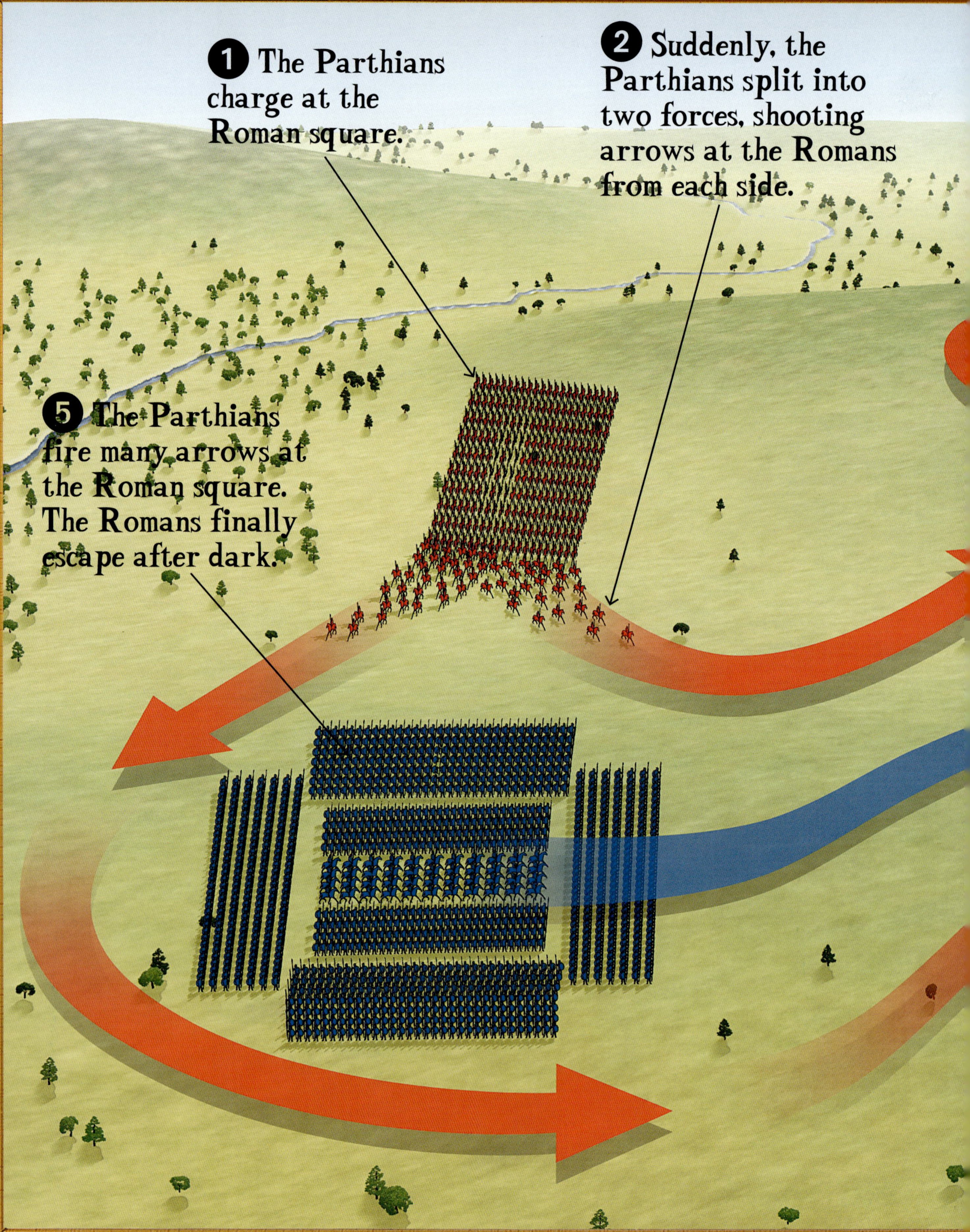
1 The Parthians charge at the Roman square.
2 Suddenly, the Parthians split into two forces, shooting arrows at the Romans from each side.
5 The Parthians fire many arrows at the Roman square. The Romans finally escape after dark.

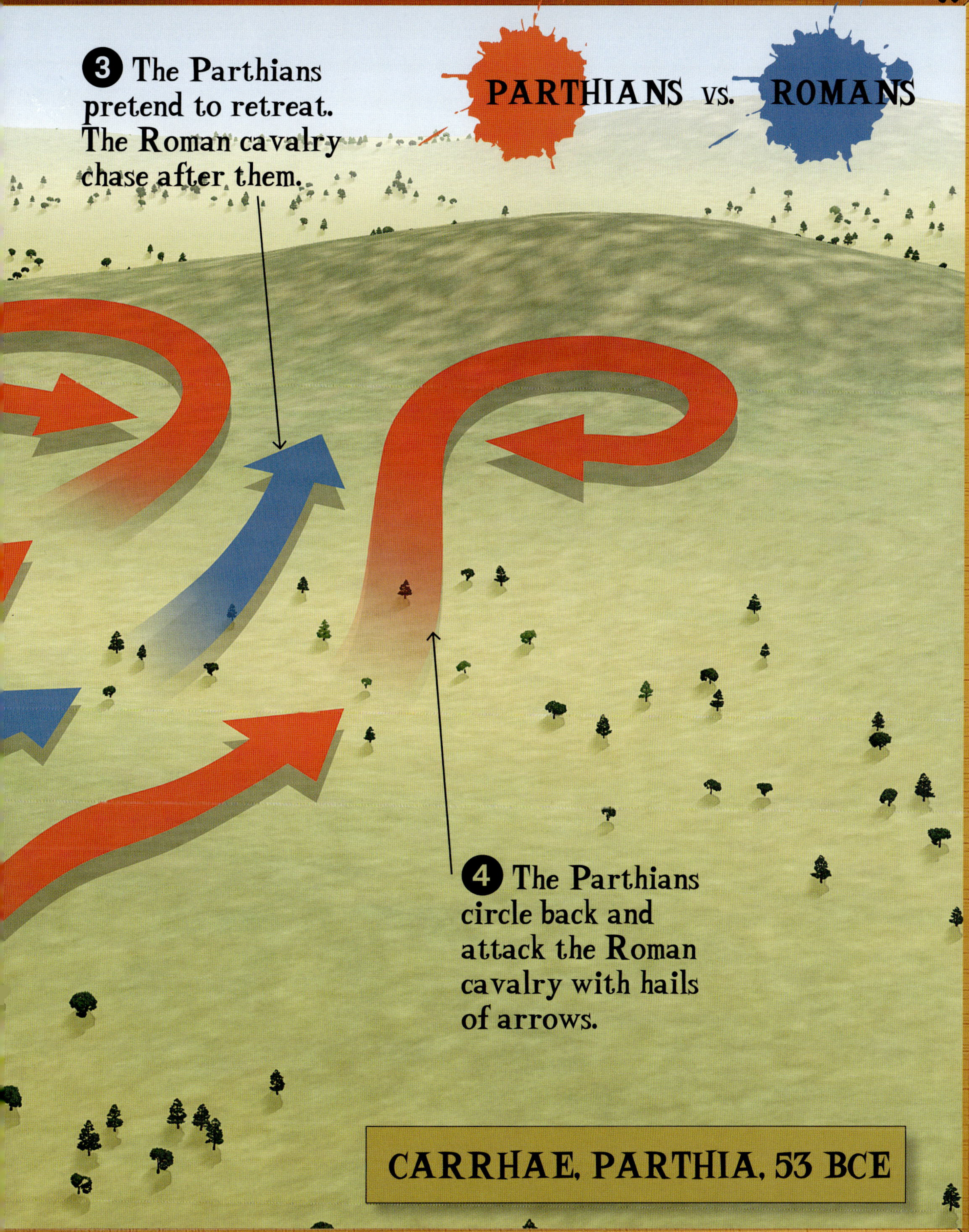
PARTHIANS vs. ROMANS
3 The Parthians pretend to retreat. The Roman cavalry chase after them.
4 The Parthians circle back and attack the Roman cavalry with hails of arrows.
CARRHAE, PARTHIA, 53 BCE

CHAPTER 3

CAVALRY AND CHARIOTS

Horses were very important in ancient warfare. A warrior on a horse or in a chariot could move faster and strike harder than one on foot.

Left: The Assyrian army used chariots to move archers to spots on a battlefield where they were needed. Assyrian chariots were light and fast.

Above: The Assyrians also used horse archers. Shooting from horseback was more difficult than from a chariot, and needed great skill.

CHARIOT WARFARE

Chariots could be used in different ways. In some armies, the warriors threw a spear or fired a bow from a moving chariot. Other soldiers jumped down to fight on foot.

Top: Chariots were made of wood, and sometimes decorated using paint and metals.

Right: This wall painting shows an Egyptian prince firing a bow from a chariot.

DID YOU KNOW?

Chariots could be pulled by horses that were not strong enough to be ridden.

FIGHTING BUGGY

Chariots had some big advantages.

- They were hard to hit with arrows because of their speed.
- They could be used to sneak round the side of an enemy.

550 – 330 BCE

PERSIAN

The Persians often used four horses to pull their large, powerful chariots.

Cutting a Path

Some Persian chariots had large blades attached to their wheels to cut up the enemy as they passed. These were called scythed chariots. The scythed chariot was manned by a crew of two – a driver and a spearman or an archer.

BEATING SCYTHED CHARIOTS

Warriors who came under attack from scythed chariots could defend themselves in a number of ways.

- **Shoot the horses or drivers with arrows.**
- **Open up gaps in the line and let the chariots go past without anyone getting hurt.**
- **Try to scare the enemy horses into turning away.**

SCYTHED CHARIOT

DID YOU KNOW?

Scythed chariots could run out of control and harm their own soldiers.

PERSIAN CAVALRY

CAVALRY POWER

Cavalry had some big advantages over chariots:

- Cavalry were more agile. They could turn quickly and react to a changing situation.
- Cavalry were easier to look after, since they had no complicated machinery to fix.
- Cavalrymen could charge close together, crushing the enemy with their power.

400 - 330 BCE

The Persian Empire lasted a very long time, and its way of fighting changed over the years. Chariots were replaced by horse archers and heavy cavalry.

Heavy Cavalry

Heavy cavalry wore armour to protect the warrior and his horse. They specialised in charging at the enemy and smashing through the battle line with swords and lances.

DID YOU KNOW?
Cavalry were more mobile than chariots – they could go places the chariots could not go.

ALEXANDER

The great warrior Alexander has often been shown on horseback, as he appears in this Greek statue.

DID YOU KNOW?
Alexander's best cavalry were called the Companions. They were skilled warriors and his friends.

THE GREAT

356 - 323 BCE

Alexander the Great was a brave warrior. More importantly, he was a skilled commander who knew how to get his troops to work together.

Combined Arms

Alexander used what we now call 'combined arms' tactics. He used his infantry to pin the enemy while his elite cavalry smashed a hole in their line with their charge.

SMART ALEXANDER

Alexander was a great general who knew how to use his warriors to best effect.

- Heavy infantry attacked the main enemy line with their long spears.
- Archers shot arrows at them.
- Cavalry protected the flanks in case the enemy tried to get around the army.

ALEXANDER'S COMPANION CAVALRY

Alexander the Great recruited his Companions from rich noblemen who could afford good horses and armour. They fought in a wedge-shaped formation, with the leaders at the front.

Lance and Sword

The Companions used a lance with a point at each end. The back end could be used to stab down at someone who was on the ground. If the lance broke, the cavalryman could fight on with half of it.

COMPANION ARMOUR

A Companion cavalryman wore a metal helmet to protect his head. He could choose what sort of body armour he wore.

- Some Companions wore a breastplate made of bronze or iron.
- Some wore leather or thick cloth body armour.
- Some preferred to wear no armour at all.

336 - 323 BCE

DID YOU KNOW?

Alexander had more than 2,000 Companion cavalry in his army.

WAR ELEPHANTS AT HYDASPES

At the battle of Hydaspes, Alexander's army was met by Indian war elephants. These creatures were frightening and hard to kill. Alexander's army opened its ranks, letting the elephants pass between its warriors, and then attacked them from the sides with long spears.

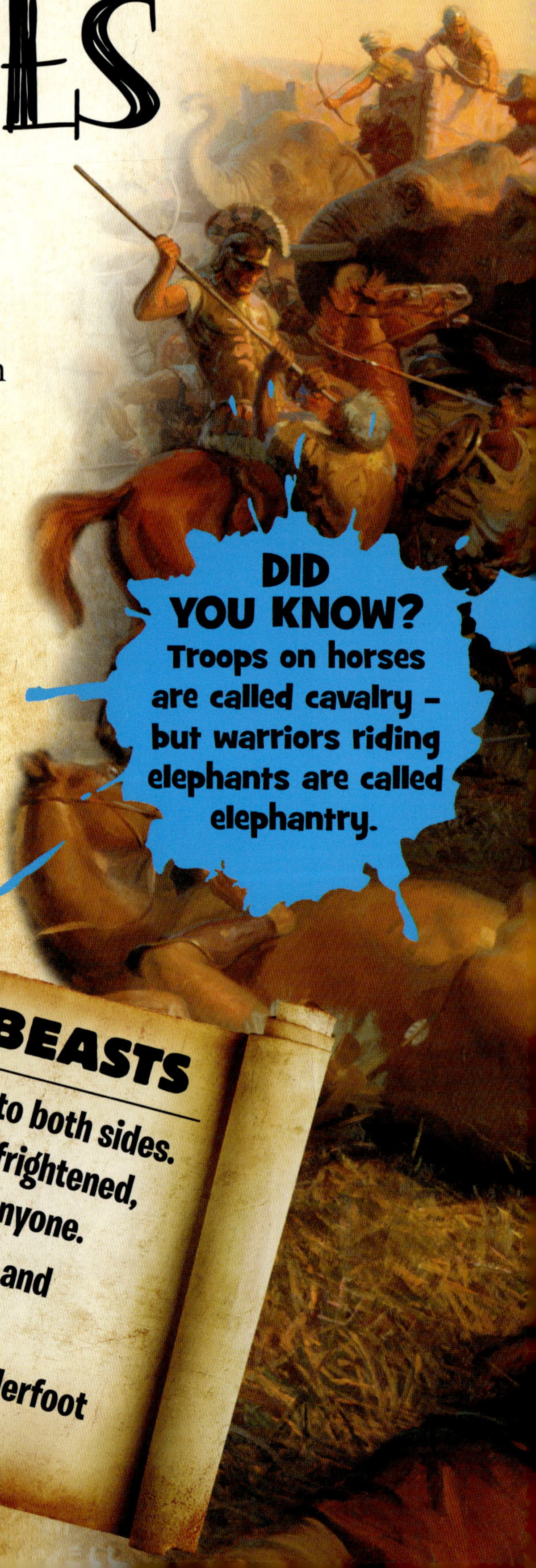

DID YOU KNOW?
Troops on horses are called cavalry – but warriors riding elephants are called elephantry.

Left: Some Macedonian coins were made to show cavalry in battle against elephants. Horses were often very frightened of the huge beasts.

DANGEROUS BEASTS

War elephants were dangerous to both sides. If the animals were wounded or frightened, they could run wild and trample anyone.

- Their riders used spears or bows and stayed out of reach of the enemy.
- An elephant could trample men underfoot or gore them with its tusks.

326 BCE

218 – 201 BCE

DEFEATING WAR ELEPHANTS

The Romans developed tactics to defeat war elephants. These included:

- using wagons with spikes on them to wound the elephants
- boiling pots of burning liquid to frighten them
- using axes to cut the elephants' legs

FIGHTING ELEPHANTS

The Carthaginians, who came from North Africa, also used African elephants in their armies. African elephants are larger and heavier than Asian ones, and this gave the fighters an advantage.

Only male elephants were used for fighting. Females were used to carry food and other supplies.

DID YOU KNOW?
The Carthaginian general Hannibal took elephants across the Alps mountains to attack the Romans.

In battle, the Carthaginians often used a type of sword called a *falcata*.

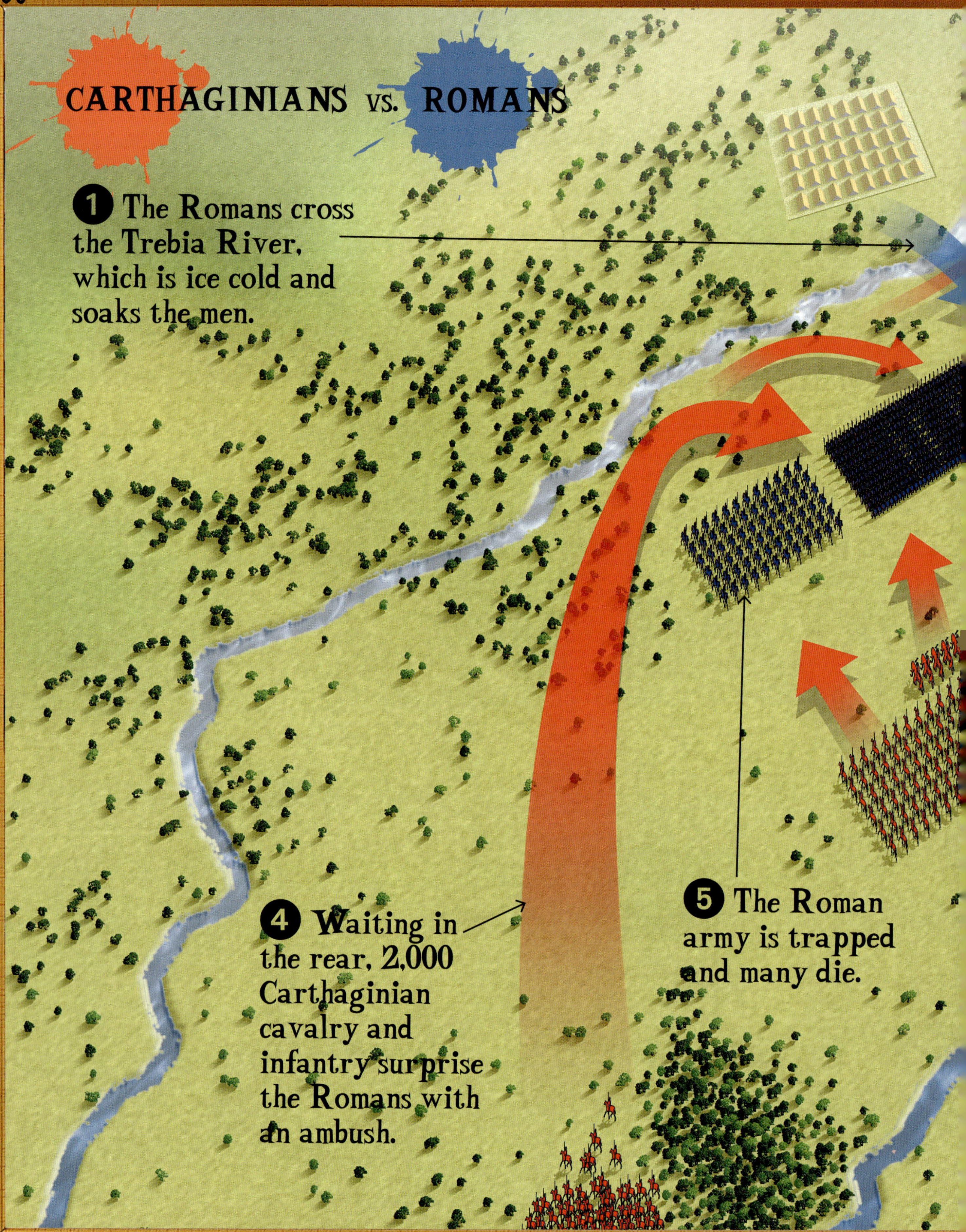
CARTHAGINIANS vs. ROMANS
1 The Romans cross the Trebia River, which is ice cold and soaks the men.
4 Waiting in the rear, 2,000 Carthaginian cavalry and infantry surprise the Romans with an ambush.
5 The Roman army is trapped and many die.

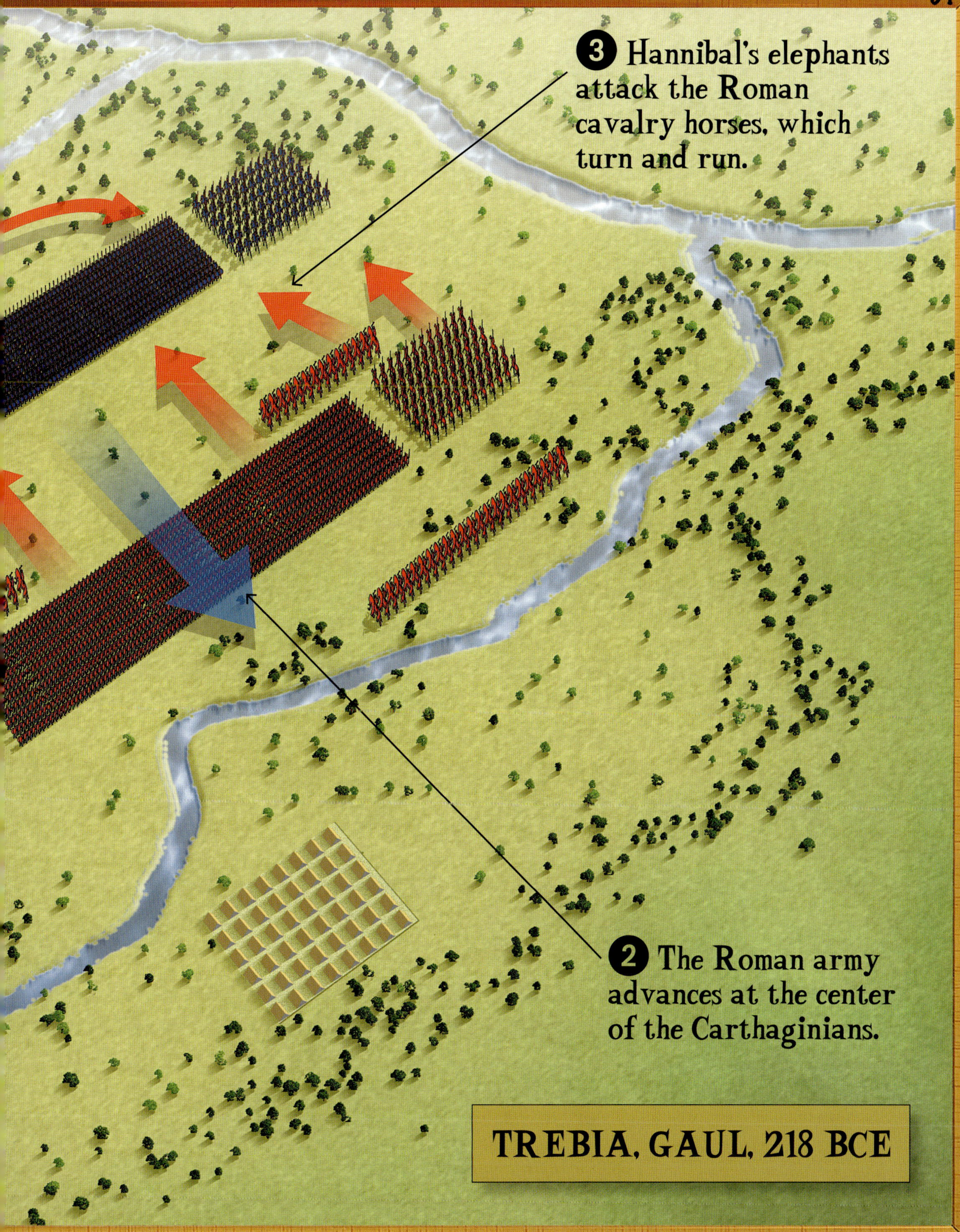
3 Hannibal's elephants attack the Roman cavalry horses, which turn and run.
2 The Roman army advances at the center of the Carthaginians.
TREBIA, GAUL, 218 BCE

300 BCE – 200 CE

ROMAN CAVALRY

The Roman army used cavalry, or *equites*, to help its legions in battle. Cavalrymen were well equipped with a spear, shield and long sword, as well as chainmail body armour.

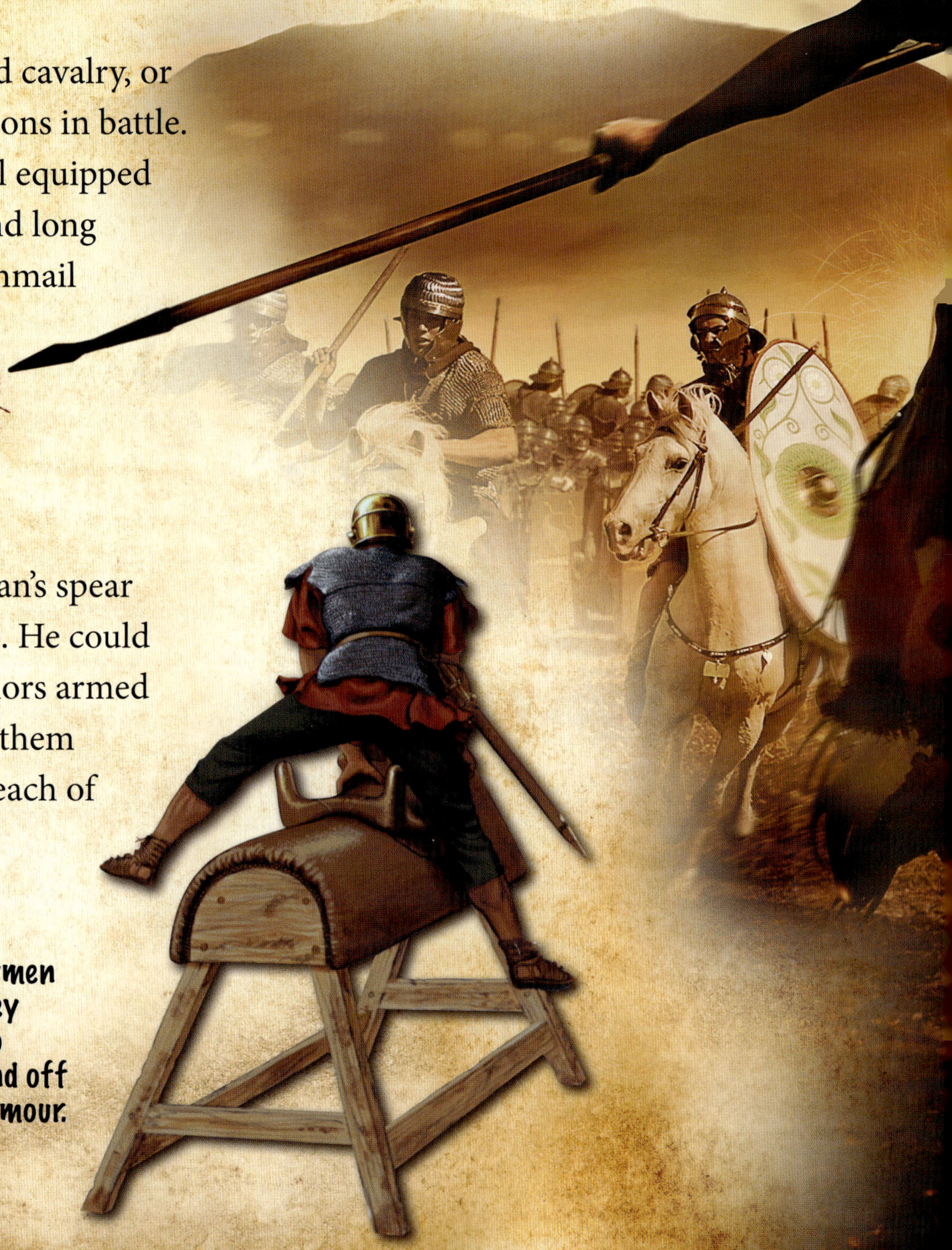

Ride-by Stabbing

The Roman cavalryman's spear gave him a long reach. He could ride past enemy warriors armed with swords and stab them while staying out of reach of their weapons.

Right: Roman cavalrymen were well trained. They used wooden horses to practice getting on and off quickly, even in full armour.

CAVALRY FACTS

- Roman cavalry used a large, round shield called a *clipeus*.
- The stirrup had not been invented in Roman times, so cavalrymen had to stay in the saddle by gripping the horse with their legs.

DID YOU KNOW?

Being a Roman cavalryman was expensive – only the richest could afford it.

BARBARIAN CAVALRY

Some barbarians were cavalry, while others rode horses to battle and then dismounted to fight. Some Celtic tribes were famous for the skills of their cavalrymen.

Cavalry Weapons

The best weapon from horseback was the long spear, or lance. A cavalryman could use a shorter spear as a lance, or throw it and then draw his sword to fight with.

HIT AND RUN

Barbarian cavalry rarely charged in a tight block at the enemy line.

- They made hit-and-run attacks against weak spots in the enemy army.
- They tried to get the enemy to chase them into an ambush.

400 BCE – 200 CE

DID YOU KNOW?
Celtic warriors dressed in bright colours and decorated their shields with artistic patterns.

CHAPTER 4

NAVAL WARFARE

Some of the most important battles in the ancient world took place at sea using ships that were rowed by their crews.

Left: Fire was an important weapon in sea battles, especially as all ships were made of wood and burned quite easily.

Above: The warships of the ancient world were called galleys. They carried a lot of rowers and a few soldiers.

GREEK SHIPS

DID YOU KNOW?
A good team of rowers could reach speeds of 13 kilometres per hour (8 mph).

GALLEYS

Galleys were built so they could attack another ship and its crew in three ways.

- They could ram a hole in a ship and sink it.
- Soldiers could shoot arrows from the deck at the enemy crew.
- If the ships came close enough, soldiers could board the other vessels.

750 - 450 BCE

The Ancient Greeks used galleys for trading, exploring and fighting. The galleys had a simple sail for catching the wind. In a fight, the sail was taken down and the rowers powered the ship.

Types of Galley

Different types of galley had different names. *Biremes* had two banks of oars, and *triremes* had three. A galley with 50 oars was called a *penteconter*.

Below: The Greek galley had a simple design. Most of the room inside was taken up with rowers.

PERSIAN FLEET

DID YOU KNOW?

The Persians had more than 1,000 ships when they invaded Greece in 480 BCE.

480 BCE

The Persian Empire fought many wars with Greece on land and at sea. Both sides built huge fleets of war galleys. These ships needed many thousands of rowers.

Fighting for the Islands

The sea between Greece and Persia was full of islands that both sides wanted to control. This led to many battles on the islands and at sea between the two sides.

SUPPLIES: The huge Persian army needed a lot of food, clothing and weapons that could only be moved by sea.

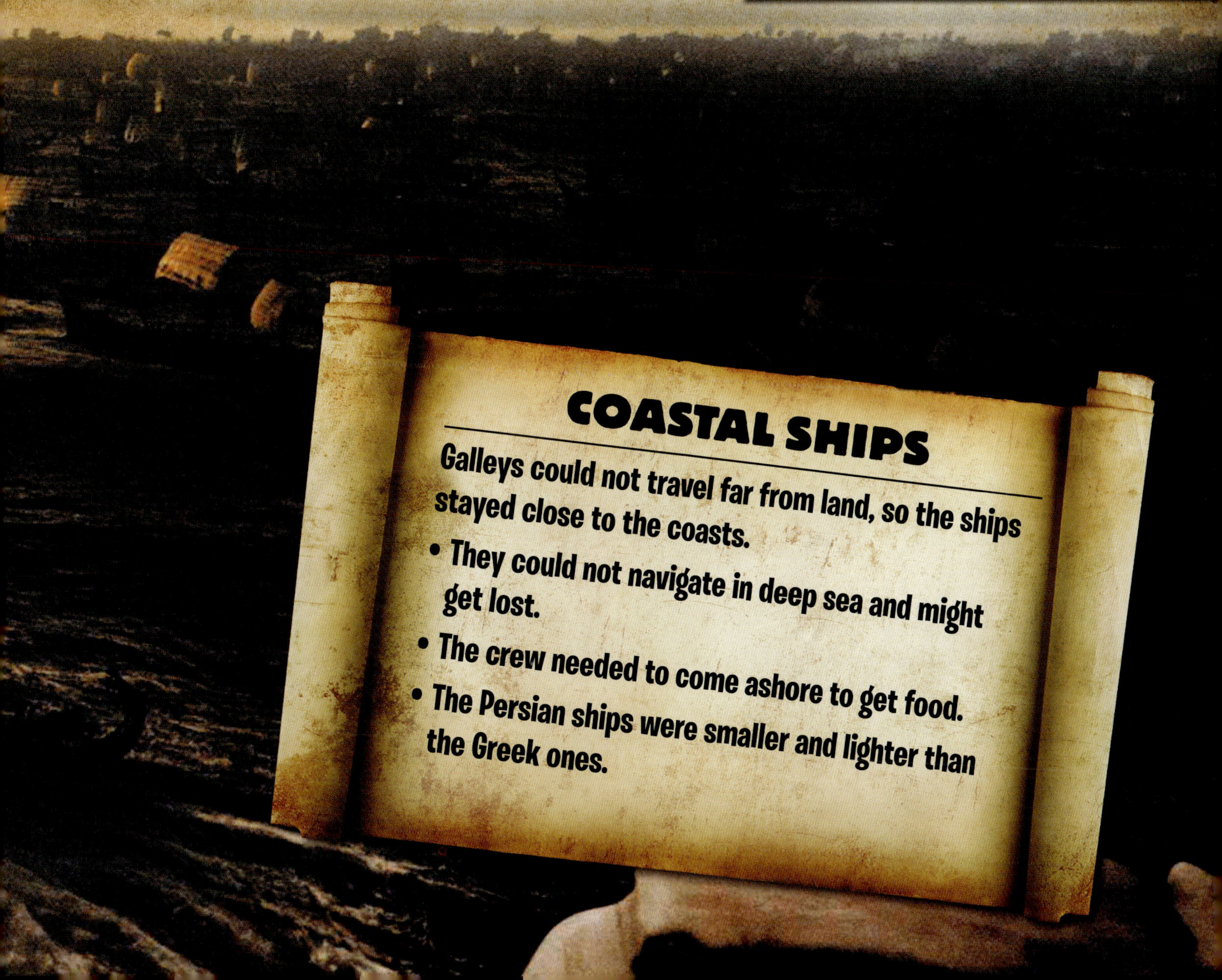

COASTAL SHIPS

Galleys could not travel far from land, so the ships stayed close to the coasts.

- **They could not navigate in deep sea and might get lost.**
- **The crew needed to come ashore to get food.**
- **The Persian ships were smaller and lighter than the Greek ones.**

480 BCE

SALAMIS

Numbering just 378 ships, the Greek fleet was badly outnumbered and hid near the island of Salamis. The Persian fleet followed them, hoping for a battle.

A ONE-SIDED FIGHT

There were so many Persian ships that they got in one another's way. The Greek fleet sank hundreds of Persian vessels and forced the rest to retreat.

The Battle of Salamis helped end the Persian invasion of Greece. Without the support of their fleet, the Persians could not press forward on land.

DID YOU KNOW?

The Persian fleet lost more than 400 ships in the battle.

GREEK–PERSIAN WARS (499–449 BCE)

The Battle of Salamis was not the end of the war. Other important battles included:

- the famous land battle at Thermopylae
- the defeat of the Persian fleet at Mycale
- the defeat of the Persians at Plataea

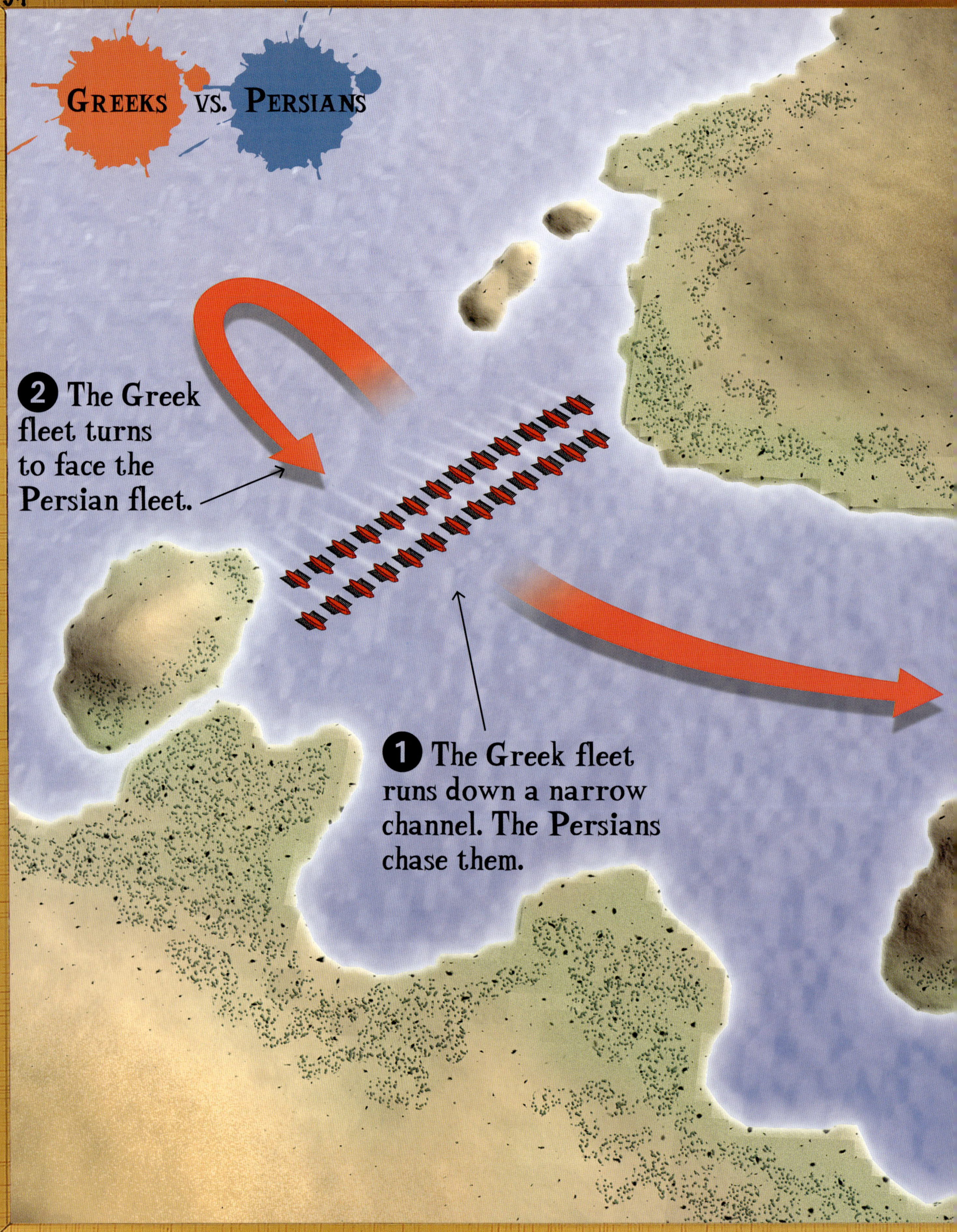
GREEKS vs. PERSIANS
2 The Greek fleet turns to face the Persian fleet.
1 The Greek fleet runs down a narrow channel. The Persians chase them.

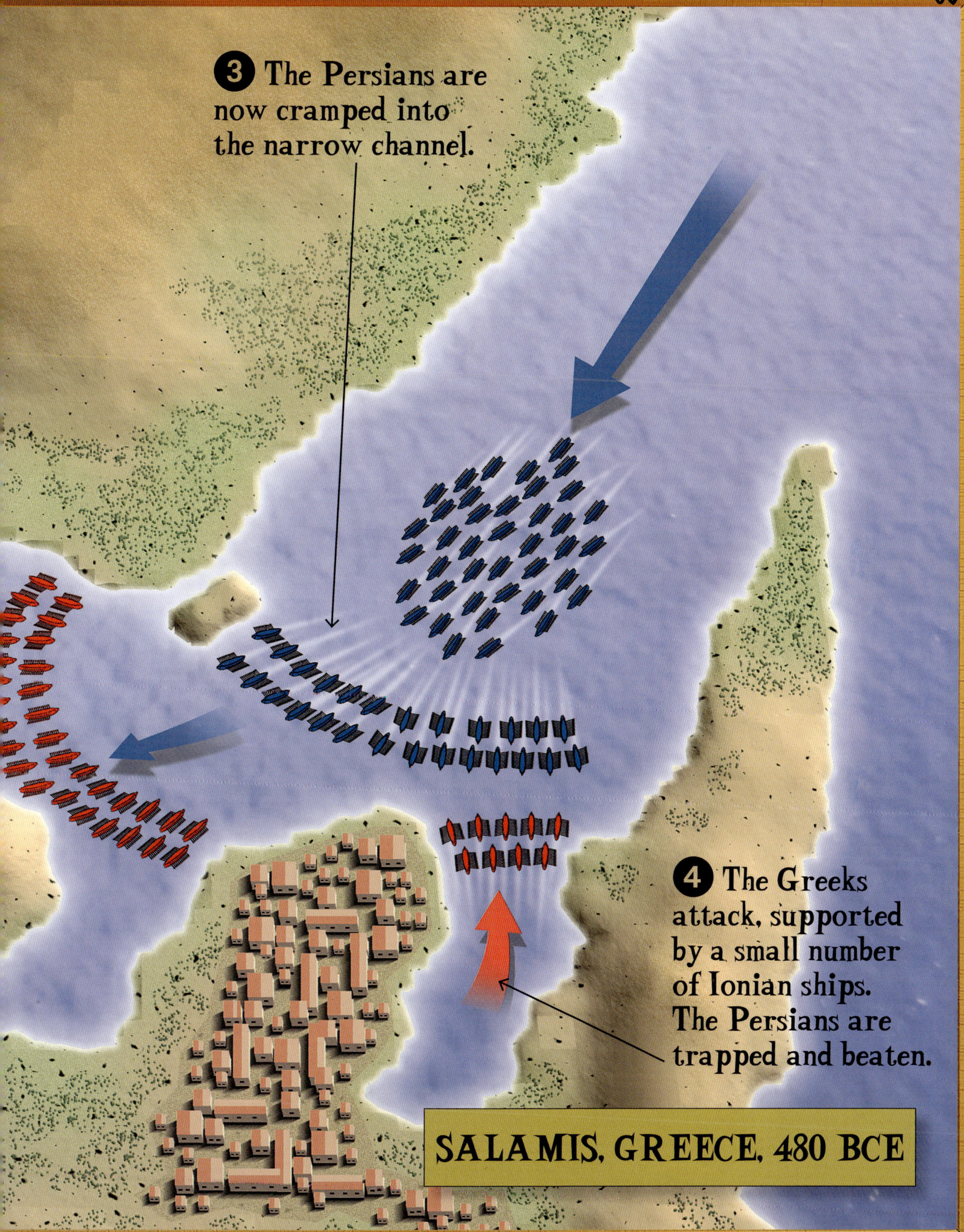
3 The Persians are now cramped into the narrow channel.
4 The Greeks attack, supported by a small number of Ionian ships. The Persians are trapped and beaten.
SALAMIS, GREECE, 480 BCE

BOARDING SHIP TO SHIP

To board an enemy ship, the attackers had to get close enough so that their warriors were able to cross to the other vessel.

Storming Aboard

The attackers had to get onto the other ship and then defeat the crew. Often the rowers would join in to defend their vessel, making it a tough and dangerous fight.

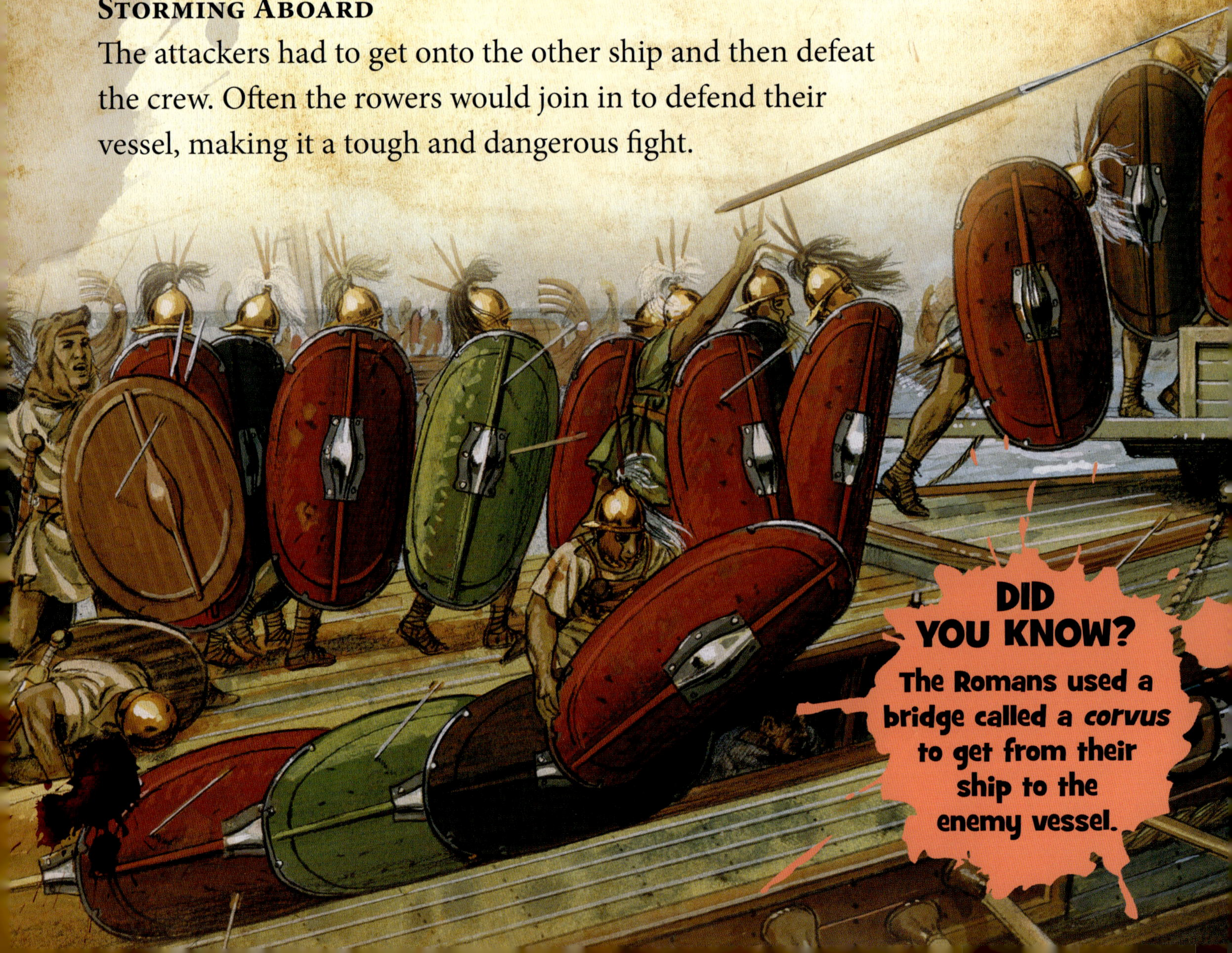

DID YOU KNOW?

The Romans used a bridge called a *corvus* to get from their ship to the enemy vessel.

BOARDING DANGERS

Boarding was difficult and dangerous. The attackers could be killed a number of ways.

- The defenders could hit them with spears and arrows.
- They could drown by being pushed into the sea.
- They could be crushed between two ships.

31 BCE ACTIUM

Some of the Roman galleys were huge and hard to board. Often, their enemies would ram these ships, leaving them helpless in the water and easy to destroy later. At the Battle of Actium, two fleets of Roman galleys fought each other. This battle was part of a war fought for control of the empire – the war between Antony and Octavian.

DID YOU KNOW?
Octavian won the battle, and became Roman emperor Augustus until his death in 14 CE.

BIG NAMES

The famous people who battled at Actium included the following:

- Mark Antony, who had helped kill Julius Caesar
- Cleopatra, Queen of Egypt and Antony's girlfriend
- Octavian, Caesar's adopted son

CHAPTER 5

CITIES AND SIEGES

Many cities in the ancient world were protected by high stone walls. Warriors had to develop special ways of attacking as well as defending these places.

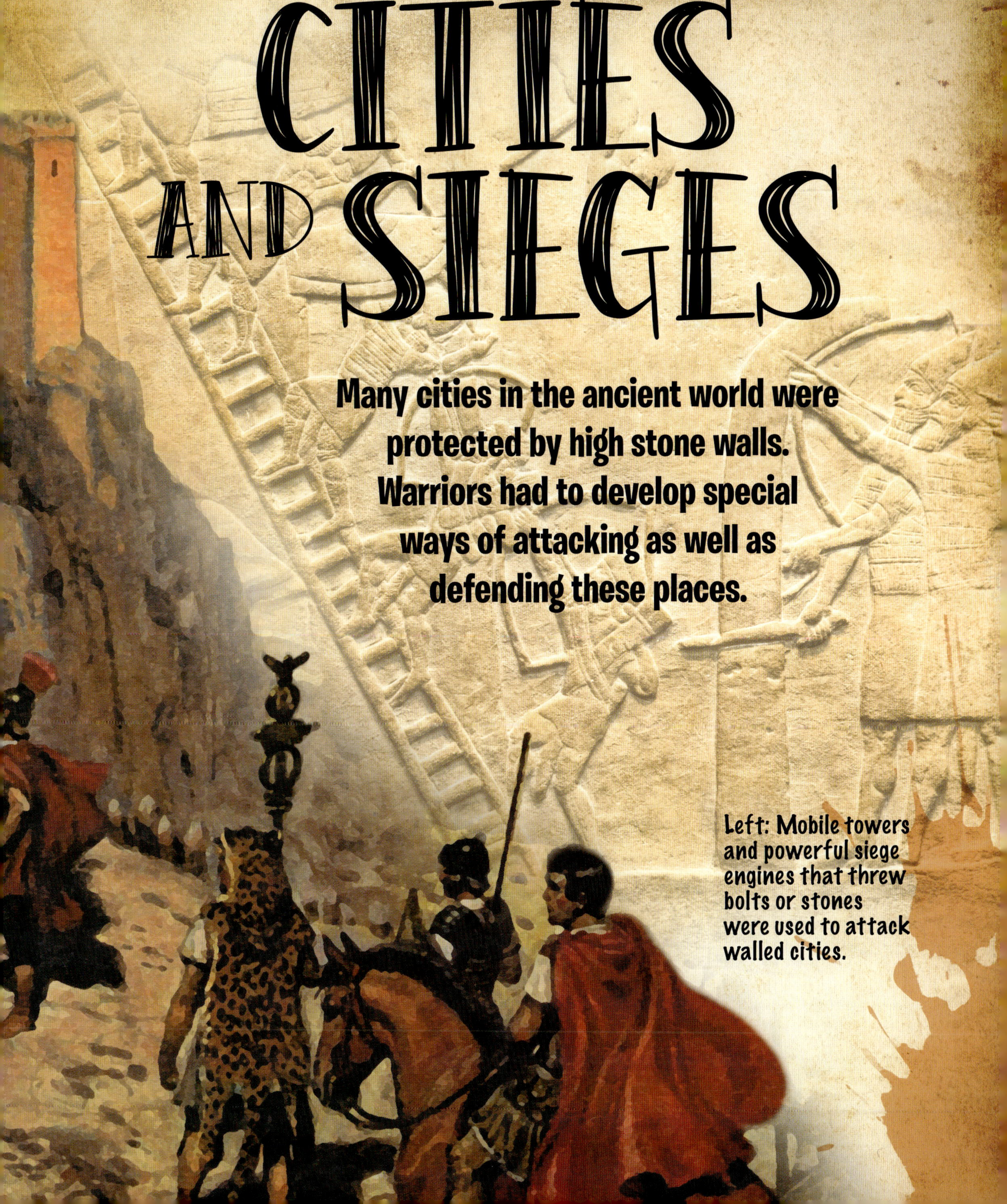

Left: Mobile towers and powerful siege engines that threw bolts or stones were used to attack walled cities.

1200 BCE

SIEGE OF TROY

DID YOU KNOW?
The ruins of Troy were uncovered in the 1870s in what is now northwest Turkey.

The film *Troy* shows how big and difficult the city of Troy was to attack.

The siege of Troy is one of the most famous battles in the ancient world. Some believe the siege may be a myth, because the only record we have is from the writings of the great Ancient Greek poet Homer.

A Long Siege

The Greeks besieged Troy for years, but they could not get inside its defences. In the end they used a trick, hiding warriors inside a huge wooden horse that they left for the Trojans as a gift.

BREAKING IN

A walled city could be defeated by:

- smashing a hole in the walls or gates
- climbing over the walls using ladders or siege towers
- sneaking inside and opening the gates
- starving the defenders to surrender

SIEGE RAMP

USING A RAMP

A siege ramp could be used several ways.

- Get warriors onto the enemy wall.
- Get siege towers close to the wall for an attack.
- Help archers shoot into the enemy city from a higher place.

DID YOU KNOW?

The siege ramp built to attack the city of Lachish 2,700 years ago is still there today.

A siege ramp was built from earth and rocks against an enemy's walls. Once it was finished, warriors could run straight onto the top of the enemy walls.

Dangerous Work

Building a siege ramp was very dangerous. The defenders would shoot arrows and throw stones at the workers, who were sometimes protected by large mobile shields.

Right: Stone carvings were made to show how siege ramps were used in attacks by Assyrian soldiers.

SIEGE TOWER

DEFEATING A TOWER

Building a siege tower took a long time, and moving it close to the enemy wall was dangerous. Defenders would try to destroy the tower by:

- setting fire to it
- tipping it over
- placing obstacles in its way

A siege tower was a tower on wheels, made to help warriors get over the wall of an enemy's city.

The tower had several floors. Warriors on the top floors could jump onto the enemy's walls or shoot arrows into the city.

DID YOU KNOW?
The towers had to be covered with something that could not be set on fire with flaming arrows.

Lower floors of the tower had siege engines, such as giant catapults. The catapults could be loaded with rocks that could be hurled into the city.

Above: One of the greatest siege towers ever built was called Helepolis. It was 40 m (130 feet) tall and was armoured with iron plates.

SAMARIA

The city of Samaria became the capital of the kingdom of Israel in 890 BCE, but was captured by the Assyrians in 722 BCE.

Three-Year Siege

The Assyrians had to besiege Samaria for three years before they were finally able to defeat its defenders. When the city fell, its people were taken into slavery.

ASSYRIAN TEAM WORK

Assyrian warriors often fought in pairs during a siege, working as a team to protect one another during battle.

- **One warrior shot his bow at the enemy.**
- **The other held a shield to protect them both.**

DID YOU KNOW?

More than 27,000 Israelites were captured after Samaria surrendered.

722 BCE

332 BCE

ATTACK FROM THE SEA

Alexander the Great besieged the Persian city of Tyre in 332 BCE. Tyre was built on an island, making it hard to attack.

Building a Causeway

The siege went on for seven months, during which time Alexander's men built a causeway, or land bridge, out to the island. This let them place siege engines where they could attack the city's defences.

ATTACK ON TYRE

Alexander's plan was to attack the city from land and sea.

- **Siege engines on the causeway attacked the walls.**
- **Catapults mounted on ships also bombarded the city.**

Right: After breaking through the walls, Alexander's men attacked from boats and stormed into the city.

DID YOU KNOW?

The defenders placed large stone blocks in the sea to keep Alexander's ships away.

SIEGE WEAPONS

DID YOU KNOW?
The longest range of a ballista was roughly 370 m (400 yards).

The Roman army used many types of siege weapons. Siege weapons were very powerful but hard to move around, so they were usually built during a siege, and broken up once the siege was ended.

BALLISTA

A ballista could fire bolts like a giant crossbow and could punch through shields and armour. Ballistas were first used in the first century BCE.

OPEN FIRE!

Siege weapons were mostly used against big targets like a city wall.

- Larger catapults hurled big rocks.
- Lighter catapults and bows fired arrows and bolts at the defenders.

SIEGE WEAPONS:
ONAGERS threw large rocks
BALLISTA fired large bolts
OXYBELES fired bolts
RAMS broke down walls

ONAGER

OXYBELES

The *oxybeles* was a Greek weapon that fired bolts. It was used from the fourth century BCE.

SIEGE RAM

52 BCE

ALESIA

Below: Fierce Celtic warriors tried to fight their way through the Roman lines at Alesia.

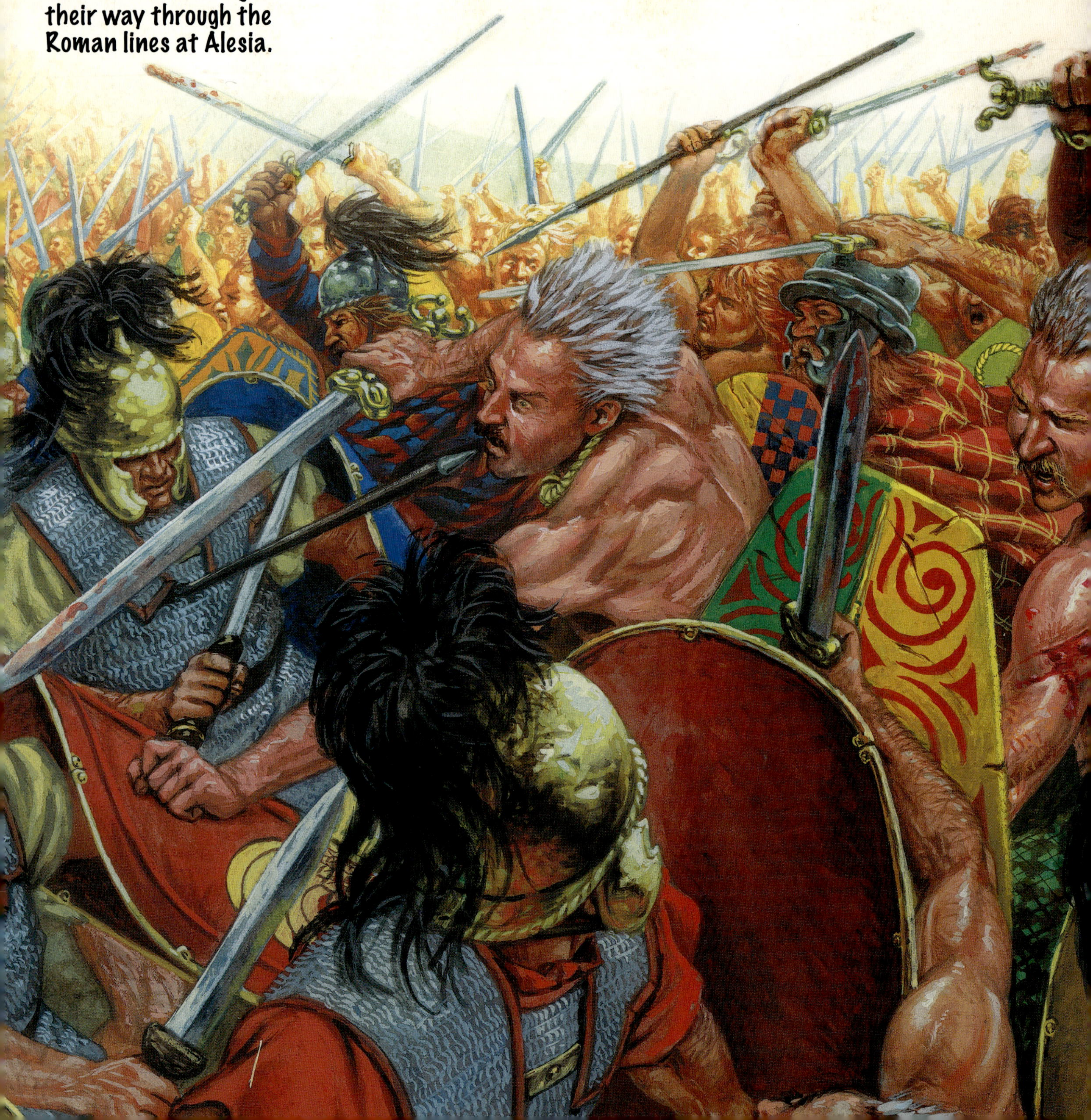

At the battle of Alesia, Roman leader Julius Caesar defeated the Celtic tribes of Gaul. The Gauls' leader, Vercingetorix, held out in the town of Alesia. The Romans besieged the town. The Romans had to defeat attacks from outside, as well as attempts by Vercingetorix to fight his way out.

DID YOU KNOW?

Julius Caesar wrote a book about his wars in Gaul, telling of his great victories.

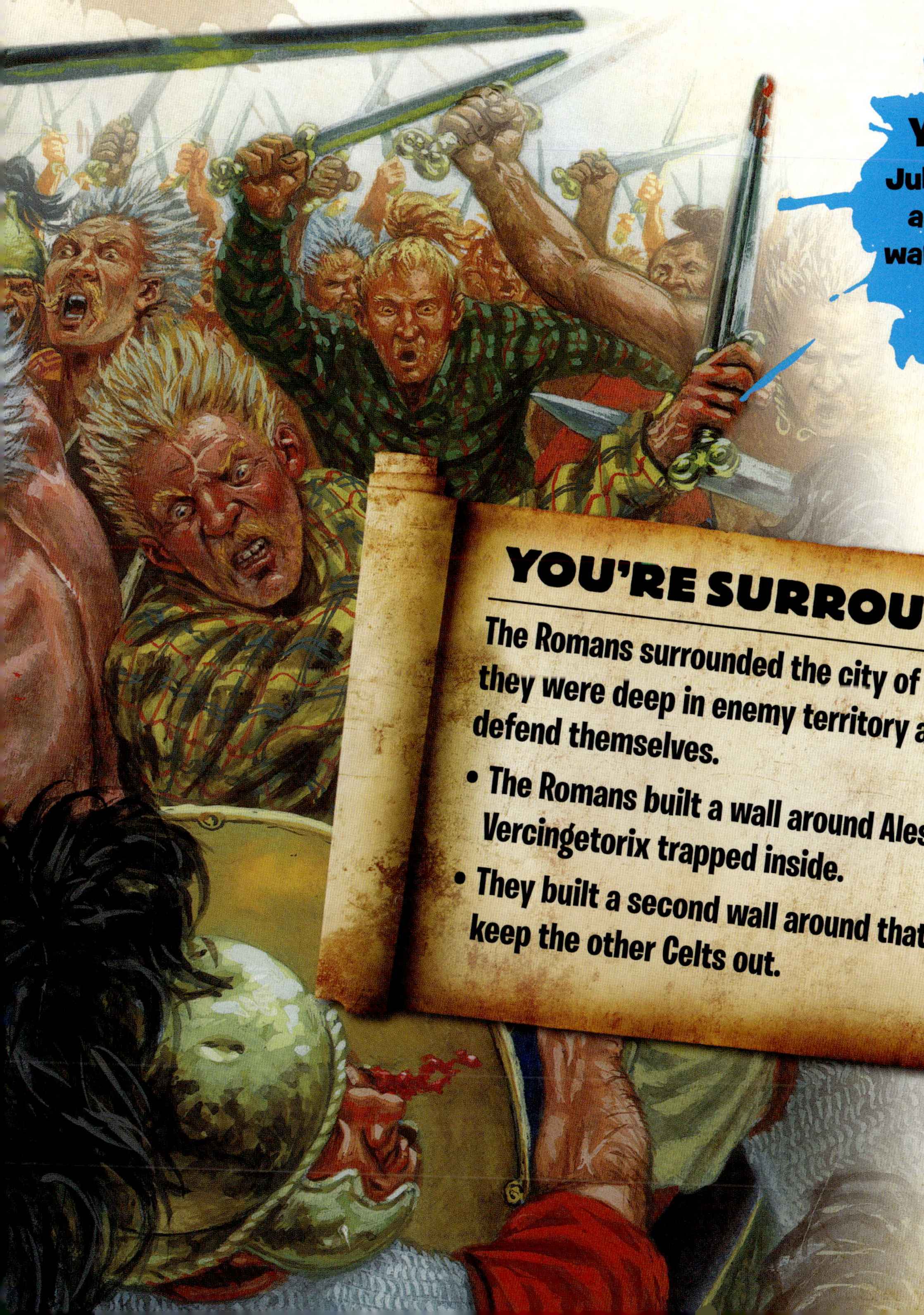

YOU'RE SURROUNDED!

The Romans surrounded the city of Alesia, but they were deep in enemy territory and had to defend themselves.

- **The Romans built a wall around Alesia to keep Vercingetorix trapped inside.**
- **They built a second wall around that one to keep the other Celts out.**

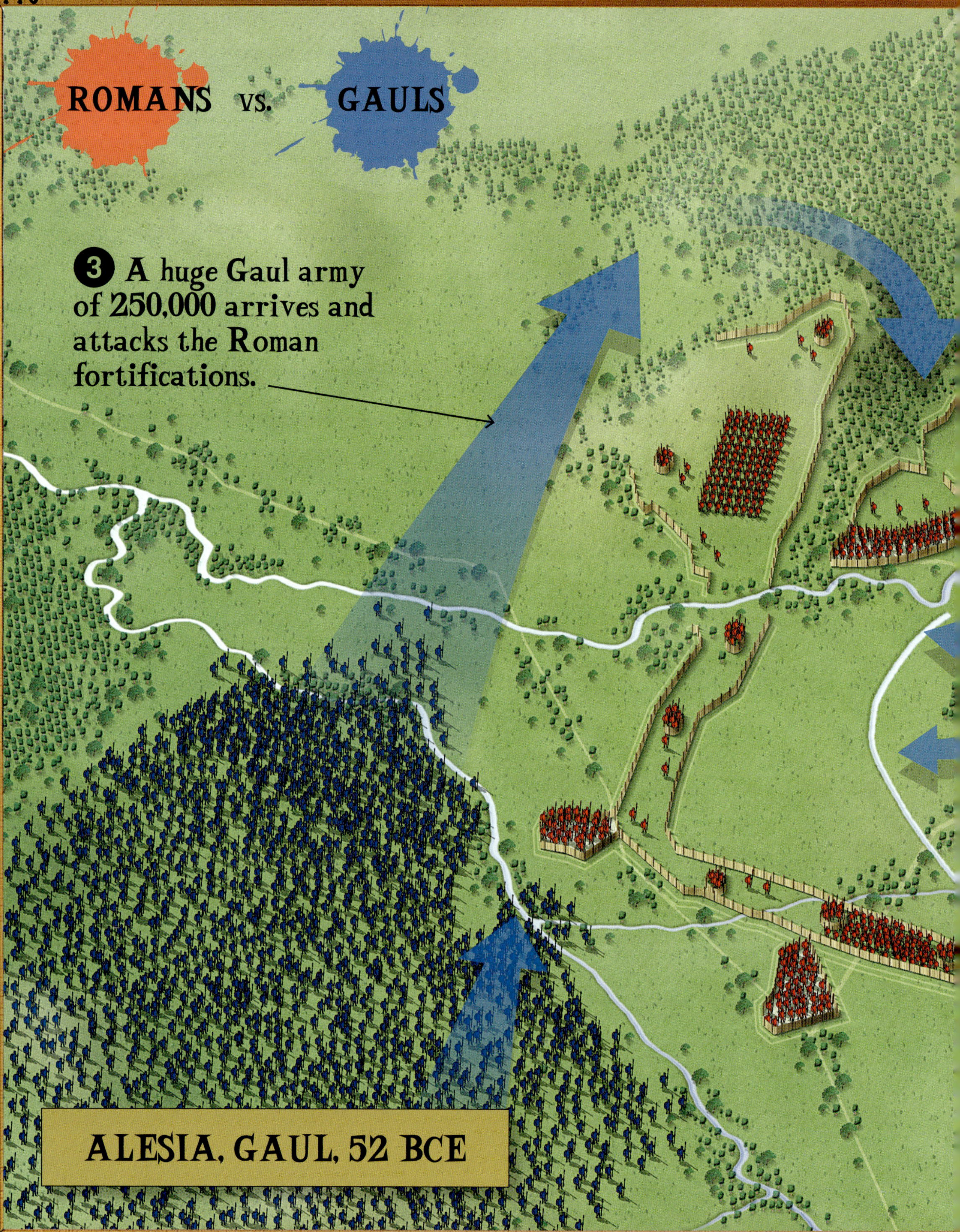
ROMANS vs. GAULS
3 A huge Gaul army of 250,000 arrives and attacks the Roman fortifications.
ALESIA, GAUL, 52 BCE

1 Vercingetorix and 80,000 Gauls hide in the hilltop fort of Alesia.
2 Caesar and the Romans build a 40 kilometre (25 mile) outer wall to trap the Gauls.
4 Gauls inside Alesia also attack the Romans.
5 The Roman fortifications prove stronger and the Gauls are defeated.

100 - 44 BCE

JULIUS

Julius Caesar was a great Roman commander who fought the tribes of Gaul and conquered them. His greatest victory was over Vercingetorix, leader of the Gaulic tribes, at Alesia.

Right: Vercingetorix (on horseback) surrenders to Julius Caesar (seated) after the battle at Alesia.

Big Changes in Rome

Rome was not an empire in Caesar's time, but his enemies feared he would try to make himself king. He was eventually killed by his enemies when back in Rome.

GREAT GENERAL

Julius Caesar was a brave commander who was well respected by his troops.

- He made sure they got enough to eat.
- He did not desert them when battles turned against them.
- He joined in some battles and fought in the front line.

CAESAR

DID YOU KNOW?
Caesar deliberately caused the war in Gaul so that he could gain power by winning it.

HADRIAN'S WALL

The Romans were very skilled at building forts and walls. The most famous Roman fortification is Hadrian's Wall, built in northern England almost 2,000 years ago. Hadrian's Wall stretches right across England at its narrowest part. Behind the wall were forts and roads used by the Roman army to defend their territory.

Right: Roman forts were like small towns, with shops, stables for horses, animal compounds and houses for people to live in.

122 - 128 CE

DID YOU KNOW?
Hadrian's Wall is 132 km (84 miles) long. It is used as a walking path today.

ROMAN FORTS

Roman forts were built the same all over the empire. They included:

- a defensive wall with gates on each side
- storehouses for grain and other food
- housing for the troops and animals
- training grounds

BATTERING RAM

WALL BUSTERS

- Some ram heads were shaped like the head of an actual ram (male sheep).
- The ram had wheels but needed flat ground to move over.

BATTERING RAM

A battering ram was a heavy weight on the end of a long pole. It was used to attack enemy walls or gates and knock them down.

DID YOU KNOW?
Rams could be protected from fire by coverings made from wet animal hides.

Swing Back, Swing Forward

The ram was suspended on ropes and pulled back by its crew. When they let go, it swung forward and slammed against the target. It might take quite a few blows to smash a hole in a wall.

Left: Some rams were mounted high up in a tower to attack the top of a wall. The tower had to be pulled into place by a large crew of slaves.

73–74 CE

MASADA

Right: The great fortress at Masada was built overlooking the Dead Sea.

DID YOU KNOW?

The 900 Jewish defenders of Masada killed themselves rather than surrender.

The Romans built a ramp and then they attacked with siege towers.

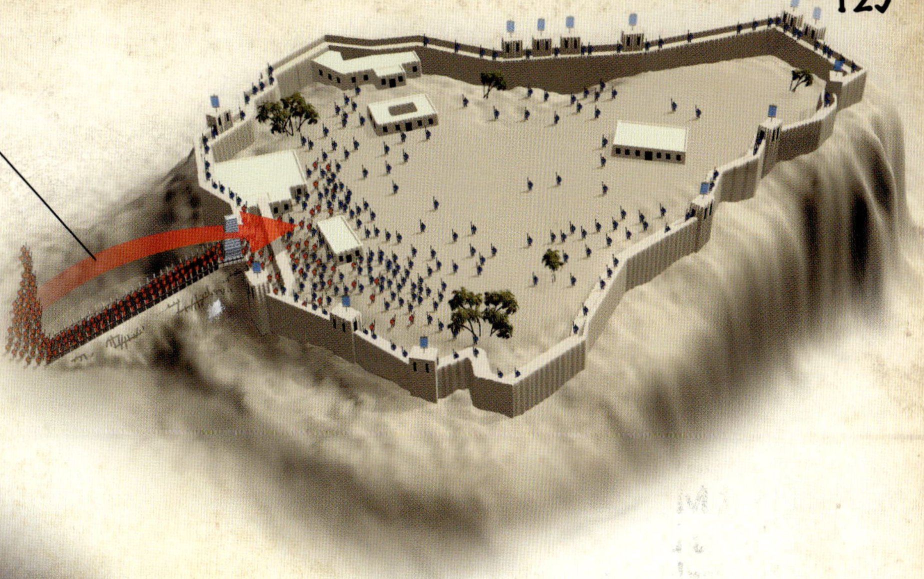

The fortress of Masada was built on the top of natural cliffs, making it extremely difficult to attack. It was occupied by Jewish warriors fighting against the Roman Empire.

The Great Siege Ramp

To attack the defenders, the Romans used thousands of slaves to build a huge siege ramp all the way up to the top of the cliffs. From there they could attack the fortress.

SIEGE TACTICS

The Roman army besieged the fortress at Masada for about a year.

- **First, they built a ramp all the way to the top of the cliffs.**
- **They brought up siege weapons and broke through the walls.**
- **Finally the Romans stormed the fortress.**

GLOSSARY

ammunition – anything that can be fired at an enemy using a sling, bow or siege weapon

Ancient Egypt – civilization based around the Nile River in northeast Africa, lasting from 3100 BCE to 332 BCE

Ancient Greece – civilization based in the eastern Mediterranean Sea that lasted from the 8th century BCE to the 6th century CE

Ancient Rome – civilization that started in Italy in the 8th century BCE and covered much of the ancient world by 300 CE

barbarians – peoples of ancient times that were not part of the great civilizations

battle standard – war flag

besiege – to surround a city and try to take it over by force

Celts – ancient people living in western Europe, including modern-day France, northern Spain and the British Isles

chainmail – armour made of small metal rings linked together

conquer – to take over something using force

elite – best and most successful

empire – lands conquered by an army for a ruler or other form of authority

equipment – special tools needed for a job, such as being a soldier

foe – an enemy

flank – the side of something

galley – low ship rowed by oars

Gauls – ancient people who lived in modern-day France

general – leader of an army

gladiator – ancient Roman fighter who put on fight performances for audiences

Greek–Persian Wars (499–449 BCE) – series of wars fought between the Greek states and the Persian empire in the eastern Mediterranean

hero – someone who is brave and does great things

ivory – main part of an elephant's tusks

lance – long spear used by cavalry

missile weapons – objects that are thrown, shot or fired

noble – person who is part of the ruling class

phalanx – group of soldiers who stand close together for defence and attack

pilum – throwing spear used by the Romans

ranks – lines of soldiers

recurve bow – bow with ends that curve away from the archer; stores more energy and can fire arrows farther than a straight bow

sarissa – long spear about 4 to 6 meters (13 to 20 feet) long

scythed chariot – chariot with sharp blades attached to the wheels

sickle – curved blade with handle

siege – when an army tries to cut off and capture a city

Sparta – city-state in Ancient Greece that was famous for its soldiers during the Greek–Persian Wars (499–449 BCE)

stirrup – one of a pair of loops for the feet attached to a horse rider's saddle to help the rider balance

tactic – plan of action for doing something

warrior – fighting person or soldier

INDEX